To Rick

CW00555310

So they say ———, ———
and laugh but they
forget the best bit: LIFT!!

I'm really grateful to have
the opportunity to train with
you and even more grateful
to be able to call you my
friend!

Happy birthday and good
luck for your 1st (of many)
competition

Dave

David M Cottrell was born in Liverpool and now lives in Lancashire with his with Ilona. He is a father of two boys, Sam and Joe. As well as writing stories he also writes songs and poems.

Dedication

To my beautiful wife Ilona and my mum Pat. Without the two of you pushing me this book would have remained on my laptop.

David Cottrell

THE 11TH HOUR

AUSTIN MACAULEY
PUBLISHERS LTD.

A CIP catalogue record for this title is available from the British Library.

ISBN 978 1 78455 028 8

www.austinmacauley.com

First Published (2015)
Austin Macauley Publishers Ltd.
25 Canada Square
Canary Wharf
London
E14 5LB

Printed and bound in Great Britain

What if by the time you realised you want to live it was already your turn to die?

This is the story of Daniel Brady. After seven years of misery following the death of his wife and infant child Daniel has decided to take his own life.

1

The day started like any other, with the buzzing of the alarm at 6:54 a.m. This may seem like an odd time but to Daniel Brady it made perfect sense. His alarm had a snooze function which was fixed at six minutes and six minutes later it would be seven o'clock on the dot. Not that Daniel was a particularly anal person, it was just that certain routines, checkpoints and considerations had become a very central part of his daily life.

Breakfast was the same, not tightly-regimented but there was certainly no need to think, "What shall I have this morning?" as almost on auto pilot Daniel reached his right arm into a cupboard containing bowls and his left into a cupboard containing cereal, had he a third arm this would probably be grabbing the milk as we speak. With the cereal poured he makes another quick reach into the cupboard with the crockery and pulls out a mug before filling and switching on the kettle.

While the kettle is boiling he sits and thumbs through a newspaper, another thing which is the same every day, the only difference here is whereas the cereal in the bowl is the same brand and flavour as yesterday it is not the exact same cereal. The paper on the other hand is the same paper he read yesterday, and the day before, the day before that and all the 2487 days prior to that also.

He sits and reads oblivious to the fact that he has read these stories time and time again; to be fair he doesn't really care. The content could be different every day and it would not make the slightest difference to Daniel, so long as the date on the front cover reads 31st May 2003 then Daniel's world is OK.

The fact that today is the date of Daniel's 34th birthday is also of no consequence to him. He knows the date is not 31st May 2003 but in this moment he wants it to be. For on 31st May 2003 Daniel woke up just like today. Alarm at 6:54 just like today. One six minute snooze just like today. Left hand retrieving the cereal in the same cupboard, just like today. Right arm retrieving the bowls. Only 31st May 2003 wasn't just like today.

It was the first day in six months he had slept for long enough to be woken by his alarm. The first time in six months he had been able to press a button to buy more time before getting out of bed. And the last time he would open his eyes to see his wife Isobel lying next to him and hear his daughter Rachel cooing in her Moses basket beside their bed.

For on 31st May 2003 Daniel's whole world came crashing down around him, when a terrible accident took the lives of his two beautiful girls. The kettle finishes boiling, he places the newspaper on the counter and makes a mug of coffee. He takes the milk to pour on the cereal and sees the two bowls standing side by side and it hits him.

Forget the fact that the coffee isn't for him, he hasn't drunk a cup of the stuff in his life, but Izzy couldn't start her day without one. Every morning it's the same, he makes it through the coffee without remembering, but that second bowl of cereal, that damned second bowl, it gets him every time.

And it's like a hammer, a sledgehammer even, hitting him in the stomach, just once but enough to knock all the wind out of him. The mug smashes to the floor, hot coffee and porcelain flying in every direction and Daniel sinking down to his knees. Later he will clean it up but for now he just weeps.

2

Daniel likes to tell himself he has got better at coping with his loss. This vicious déjà vu still plays out each and every morning but once he has endured this initial outburst he is often able to go on to have a perfectly normal, if not a little detached day.

This was not the case at first but over time he has made it possible to return to work, have friends and to the rest of the world seem like a perfectly normal person. He rides the bus, he works his 9-5, he meets his deadlines and he even goes to the occasional group lunch or staff party. To the rest of the world he would at worst seem a little shy, nothing to indicate the grief with which he still lives.

In fact he had even happened to have a fairly limited love life. Around four years after his loss a girl called Tara had started working in his department. He was 31 at the time and she was only 24. She asked him to go for drinks one night after work and told him that she was very focused on her work but sometimes just needed to let her hair down. This worked perfectly for Daniel so they started seeing each other casually.

Things were going great for a while; Tara had her own place where they could spend the evening and make love so Daniel never had to betray the memory of his wife by taking anyone else to their home. The problems came around six months in when Tara began questioning why Daniel would never spend the night. She had a one bedroom flat so no annoying housemates to get in the way and he seemed perfectly happy to be in her bed, just so long as he didn't fall asleep there.

Daniel didn't know how to explain, in fact he didn't even want to. His morning was his and his alone and he didn't expect that anyone could ever understand that. So he broke it off and hasn't dated anyone since.

This is possibly the biggest talking point anyone has about him. The office has had a pretty quick turnover of staff of late and only a couple of members of senior management and the strange man who works in the mail room that never composes full sentences when speaking were still at the company seven years ago.

So instead of "Oh poor Dan, he lost his wife and child at such an early age", the conversations were more like, "Have you noticed Dan never seems to go on any dates? Do you think he's gay?"

Daniel had heard this inane chit chat on more than one occasion and his attitude was firmly "let 'em talk". Chances are most of them will have left the company or been fired before long anyway.

No, he was happy to let them think whatever they liked, he knew himself and that was all that mattered. He would try his best not to get too involved with this sort of conversation, though it seemed inevitable that he would have to listen to it, or at least appear to listen to it on a daily basis. This was thanks to a man called Johnnie DeLance, one of the four other people Daniel had the joy of sharing a desk with.

Johnnie was the kind of guy who needed to be, or at least appear to be involved in everything. Every conversation was an anecdotal account of some kind of social event and it would seem to everyone else that Johnnie had an almost endless supply of friends. He would love nothing more than to constantly brag about where he had been the night before or who had invited him to some exclusive party that was sure to be "off the chain".

Today was certainly no exception to this. It was around 10:30 and Daniel had just got back to his desk after pouring himself some cordial in the small kitchenette located off the rear of the office. No sooner had he sat down, Johnnie had wheeled over in his chair with a juvenile grin on his face.

"Oh, mate," he said, although when Johnnie said mate it always sounded like it had at least seven As in it. "You would not believe the time I had last night."

Daniel had gotten his "conversations" with Johnnie down to a fine art now and knew that providing he gave him a cursory glance before returning his gaze to his screen, and occasionally chirped in with a monosyllabic affirmation here and there, Johnnie would to all intents and purposes believe he had Daniel's full attention. With this in mind he merely said, "Hmmm?" and cast his attention back to his work.

"Yeah, man," Johnnie continued. "Well I went to this party with Kim from HR, and while we were there we met this guy who owns like twelve limo companies, and you're not gonna believe who is one of his regular clients..."

Daniel saw his cue and mumbled a quick, "Who?" but instead of returning his attention to his screen he found himself distracted by something across the office. Mr Framer, Daniel's line manager was stood in the doorway of his office talking to a very important-looking man wearing what Daniel could tell even from across the office was a very expensive suit. Mr Framer was making some gestures and pointing across the office, but what really attracted Daniel's attention is that he caught him pointing straight at where he and Johnnie were sat chatting.

He felt a strange sensation come over him and it was almost as if the only one of his senses that was still working was his sight. It was as though cotton wool had been wrapped around his ears, everything was muffled. Even time seemed to stretch out as the office around him seemed to carry on in a reticent slow motion.

"Yo, are you listening to me, man? Dan, Dan, DAN!"

Dan snapped back to the conversation and for once found himself actually contributing a full sentence. "Sorry, Jon, what were you saying?"

"I was just telling you about this limo driver, man..." Johnnie tailed off and a quizzical look took over his face. "Hey are you OK? You don't look so good."

What was unusual about this, even more than the fact that Daniel had never known Johnnie to ask about how someone else was feeling, was that Daniel was sweating profusely and he hadn't even noticed it himself. He excused himself from the conversation and headed hurriedly for the bathroom.

Although the rest of the office had recently gone through a serious re-modernisation it would appear that the bathrooms had been way down on the to-do list. Though by no means a shambles they were still seriously dated, with individual freestanding porcelain sinks complete with old-fashioned individual hot and cold taps. A point which often surprised Daniel as with how much the company was cutting back expenditures these days he thought more modern taps which could not be left running would save a few extra pennies when the utility bills came in.

In this instance however he was glad of the antique design; he set the cold tap running and slumped over the sink, staring at himself in the mirror and trying to focus on the sound of the running water. After sixty seconds or so he rinsed his face with the water, rubbing his eyes firmly in an attempt to shake this uneasy feeling from his gut. He didn't know what had come over him and even the shock of the cold water on his face seemed unable to have any positive effect.

At that moment he was startled as the door swung open and Framer came walking in. "Brady," he said effusively and gave him a nod before positioning himself in front of one of the urinals. "Everything OK? You look a little flushed." Framer gave himself an approving chuckle, clearly pleased with his hardly Shakespearian wordplay.

"I'm fine, boss," he said. "Was just feeling a little clammy at my desk. It's uncharacteristically warm for March wouldn't you say?"

Framer grunted in a way that let Daniel know he didn't buy his story. Daniel felt a new wave of uneasiness wash over him and wasn't sure if this was more to do with some deep rooted paranoia based on the encounter he had just witnessed between Framer and the man in the suit, or the fact that Framer was choosing to have this conversation whilst he was urinating, an act Daniel considered as very private, being the kind of person who would always choose the stall over the urinal.

Framer finished his business and moved to the sink next to Daniel. Daniel caught himself wondering if Framer's washing his hands was merely a formality for Daniel's benefit. He had always seemed a more "get in – get out" kind of guy.

"I'd like to see you in my office this afternoon, if that's

OK, Daniel," Framer said. "Nothing to worry about and no real rush, just pop in when you get a spare moment."

He dried his hands on his trousers and left as abruptly as he had entered. Nothing to worry about Daniel thought. But the strange thing is Framer always referred to everyone by their surname. In all his time working under him he had never known him to use anyone's first name. Daniel tried to cast this thought to one side, as this unusual feeling did not require any further fuelling. He went back to his desk, put his headphones on and focused on his work until shortly after midday.

Another one of his little routines was lunch. He would take it at promptly one p.m. every day. Everyone in the office knew this so they didn't even bother scheduling meetings involving him at this time. Today however the residual feeling of the morning's events was still leaving him uncomfortable so he decided to head out early just before 12:30.

The offices were located a short walk from the high street, convenient enough to get to one of the local shops or cafés to get some lunch but just far enough to be outside the pay and display zone; heaven forbid the managers would have to get public transport or pay for parking!

Daniel meandered down to the high street trying to catch hold of his thoughts. He walked past Prêt a Manger and Greggs before entering in to JC's an old fashioned greasy spoon café that had somehow survived the influx of American style coffee houses that had swept the area in the late 90s.

JC stood for Jeannie Crompton, the proprietor and namesake of the café who had owned it since the mid 70s and still worked there every day, despite rapidly approaching her 60th birthday. As a regular of the café she recognised Daniel instantly and she smiled and shouted, "Good afternoon, Daniel," as he entered the room.

It wasn't much to look at but JC's was a little home from home for Daniel and had been for as long as he could remember. He considered Jeannie to be one of his only friends actually. Not that they would ever spend time together in any other capacity than café owner and customer, but she was the only person he felt comfortable talking about Izzy to. Even on the rare occasions he spoke to his parents this subject was taboo, but Jeannie somehow got a free pass.

This may be down to Daniel and Izzy spending some of their time in there together consistently throughout the course of their relationship. From the day Izzy had challenged him to take her out on a date for only £5 it had become "their spot" and no matter where they ended up in their walk of life they would always wind up back at that grubby little café on the corner of Hove Street.

This was a big deal for Daniel, this was his one o'clock ritual, only today it was 12:30, a fact which did not go unnoticed by Jeannie. "Little early today aren't we, hun?" she said while setting down a glass of fresh orange juice in front of him.

"Yeah, just needed to get out of the office," he replied.

"Everything OK?"

"Yeah…" He hesitated. "You ever get a feeling just come out of nowhere that just leaves you feeling uneasy? And you just can't place your finger on why?"

"Not since my divorce in '86," she joked. "But seriously I know what you mean and in my experience it always works out to be my imagination running away with me. Now what can I get you today?"

The question was unnecessary as every day Daniel had the same thing. Two slices of brown toast with two sausages a fried egg and a small helping of baked beans. The meal had been on special on that first date with Izzy and had allowed him to even splash out for a cup of coffee for her whilst staying within the budget.

"You're probably right," he concluded and then gave her his order. He didn't find it impersonal that she had asked, as he knew her motives weren't that of carelessness but of a mutual understanding that though he would probably never change he still had the right to.

He looked out of the window and watched the world go by and by the time his food arrived he had truly let go of the dread of the morning. He used the toast, the sausage and the egg to make a sandwich and settled in to enjoy the remains of his lunch hour.

3

Walking back to the office he allowed his mind to drift to much more enjoyable things. He was a big sci-fi and horror fan and waiting for him at home was a copy of Dean Koontz's latest offering, which although he was only 46 pages into Daniel had already decided was an instant classic. To a certain extent he had grown to, if not enjoy, at least acknowledge his solitude and take small comfort in another of his little routines.

His mood well and truly lifted, he walked back into the office and returned to his desk merely to drop off his jacket before heading straight for Framer's office. Best to tackle these things directly, he thought to himself.

Framer's office had a window with vertical blinds which looked out onto the main workspace. The blinds were drawn firmly but the door was wide open. Framer had a pretty decent open door policy which meant if the door was open then come on in. Daniel gave a courteous knock on the door anyway before edging his way inside.

"Brady!" Framer said energetically. He was using the surname again, surely a good sign Daniel thought. "Come in and have a seat."

Daniel closed the door and moved further into the office. He was just about to sit down when he saw Framer had a sandwich sat half eaten on some tin foil on the desk.

"Oh, you're having your lunch, boss, shall I come back later?"

"Don't be absurd, boy! You know if the door's open then…"

"Come on in!" Daniel finished his sentence for him and they both chuckled, though Daniel's laugh was more of nerves than anything else.

This was the kind of banter Framer liked and secretly Daniel enjoyed taking part. What he wasn't so keen on was Framer's referring to him as "boy". Daniel had long considered himself a man, but the more condescending fact was that Framer was only four years his senior. On the whole he was a good manager despite his bathroom etiquette, but little things like this cast him in an extremely arrogant light.

"So you wanted to see me, boss?"

"Yes, son." Another of his patronizing terms. "First off I just wanted to thank you for the work you did on the February reports. Very detailed and ahead of schedule as always."

"Thank you, sir," Daniel said with a hint of pride.

"I don't know if you've noticed," Framer continued, "but recently a lot of staff have been getting moved around, not just internally, but also a few off to our head office in London."

"Actually, sir, I thought they were just being let go, poor economy and all that..." Another nervous laugh.

"Quite..." Framer said with an uncomfortable look on his face.

Before he could carry on Daniel starting talking again. "In fact, sir, I think subconsciously I must have thought the same fate was to happen to me when I saw you talking with that man in the suit this morning. You'll forgive me for misleading you earlier, but that was the real reason I was in the bathroom, and that was even after you assured me it's nothing serious."

Daniel realized he was rambling uncharacteristically and what was more, the clamminess had returned. He stopped talking immediately and swallowed hard.

The expression on Framer's face grew suddenly very serious, which had the effect of instantly tying Daniel's stomach into knots.

"Well... there is something we need to talk to you about..." He left a long, uncomfortable pause before continuing. "But I can assure you that you still have a place in the company, if you want it that is?"

"Of course, sir, I have worked and been loyal to this company my entire adult life. You're as close as family to me." This hyperbole made true simply by the fact that Daniel was not actually close to his actual family.

"Well that's great, but you should probably hear what we are offering first."

Daniel felt quite sheepish and resisted the urge to sink down into his chair. Framer took another bite of his sandwich and continued speaking with his mouth full, another deplorable trait in Daniel's eyes.

"You see, Dan," there's that first name again, "the big wigs over at head office have decided to downsize our little operation over here, as you said earlier, poor economy and what have you." Dan should be focusing on the words, but the blob of mustard in the corner of Framer's mouth is stealing the show, he forces his gaze to meet Framer's and fights desperately to focus on what's important here.

He realizes he must have missed a sentence or two as it takes him a second to get the conversation back into context. "Now I've always been fond of you," Framer says, crumbs flying out in all directions, "and so when head office said they were needing to downsize but required a few key members of staff for a different project, and for me to recommend some of my more exceptional employees, then of course you were the first on my mind."

Daniel saw straight through this corporate bullshit, his feeling earlier was right, he was being hung out to dry but without the decency of just coming out and saying it here was Framer doing the old carrot on a string routine. Daniel continued to listen to what he had to say, but his heart was no longer in it.

"So, what we are proposing is that, as one such exceptional individual, you would like to move to a place in the Sales Operations department in the head office in London."

Framer was grinning like a Cheshire Cat, and Daniel caught a stray bead of sweat forming on his manager's forehead. Framer was nervous, Daniel could see he had practiced this little speech up until this point, but now he was sailing without a navigator.

"So let me get this straight," Daniel started impudently, "you want me to just up sticks and move my life to London?"

The fact that Daniel's "life" was nothing more than a few lonely routines was beside the point, he did not like being given ultimatums.

Framer could sense the rage building in Daniel's voice and immediately jumped in on the defensive. "But I'm trying to do you a favour here, Brady, the salary is better and the advancement opportunities are much greater than what they are here, try to think of it as a new opportunity."

"Spare me the 'friend' act, you and I both know you sold me out here and now you're just trying to appease your guilty conscience."

With his efforts to placate Daniel squashed Framer now chose a more aggressive standpoint. "Come on, Daniel, be reasonable, I could have just laid you off, but I didn't, and as for the relocation it's not exactly as if you have a life here, not since…" Framer hesitated.

"Go on, say it." Daniel was incensed.

"Nothing."

"Say it, you piece of shit! Finish your goddamned sentence."

"Since the incident… with Izzy and the baby."

That insolent little bastard, Daniel thought. He could feel the blood boiling inside him and he decided that the only answer to a slap in the face such as he had just been served was a punch in the teeth for the shit that served it. In a flash he was out of his chair and lunging across the desk, fist clenched and teeth bared. He planted a single right hook square on Framer's jaw and in that instant he was flooded with an unbelievable amount of feelings.

First the satisfaction of the punch landing, it was almost euphoric. Surprisingly this came before pain that shot straight through his arm as two of his knuckles shattered on impact. Next came the relief as the bubble of rage suddenly popped. He had never lashed out like this in his life, not even at the bastard who fled the scene of his wife's crash and later got off all charges on some shitty clerical error made during the time of his arrest. Finally came the shame, sure he had struck out defending Izzy's honour, but she would never have wanted this, to see her beloved Dan-Dan reduced to a Neanderthal, thinking only with his fists. For the second time that day he dropped to the floor and wept.

For a moment Framer was stumped, the aching in his jaw paled in significance to the confusion in his head. His natural instinct at first was to strike back, but here he was faced with a man sat kneeling on his office floor, a broken and crying man, who Framer could not deny he himself had most likely tipped over the edge. He took a moment to compose himself, then stood up and went around the desk to where Daniel was collapsed on the floor.

"Dan," he said, still keeping a fairly safe distance. "Dan." This time moving a little closer. "Dan." For this attempt he reached out to grab Daniel's arm.

Dan abruptly brushed him away and slowly started rising to his feet. "Keep your hands off me, you pig!" This was more breathed out than spoken. "I have nothing more to say to you."

Framer held his arms out wide in protest but Daniel didn't even raise his eyes to see. He turned and headed out into the main office shuffling his steps in an almost zombie-like state. He moved through the workspace as if being guided by some unseen force. Everyone else had heard the majority of his altercation despite the closed door and now they stared on as if some celebrity had just sauntered through the office.

Dan moved through the mass of onlookers with only two goals in mind, get the photo of him, Izzy and Rachel that was sat on his desk and then get the hell out of there. He did all of this without stopping or pausing once. Johnnie thought about piping up to see if he was alright but for once even he was lost for words. Dan's exit from the office was met without a single syllable uttered by anyone and it wasn't until the door swung shut behind him that the office gossip engine kicked back into full swing.

4

Though longer in duration, Daniel's journey home was just as much a blur as his trip through the office. Having walked this route five days a week for pretty much forever it was no mean feat to complete it on auto pilot. The roads that needed crossing were all small and residential, hardly any traffic in the middle of the afternoon and there were no schools or nurseries on the route which made it uncommon that he would pass more than a handful of people.

He arrived back at his house a little before four p.m. and before even taking his shoes or jacket off he flopped onto the couch, holding his beloved family picture in his hands.

As he stared into Izzy's eyes he found himself talking out loud. "Why? Why? Why? Izzy." He started crying again. "Why do they want to take me away from you, from here, our house? Why can't they just let us be together?"

But they weren't together, they hadn't been for more than half a decade, and even through all his delusions, of this fact Daniel was painfully aware.

They say that often in our darkest hour a moment of clarity can unexpectedly find us and this is exactly what happened to Daniel as he sat there weeping on the afternoon of his 34th birthday. As if by some sort of divine providence (although Daniel did not believe in such things) all of the synapses in Daniel's brain started firing, locked together in one simple but very potent thought. "If they want to stop us being together, then I'll make it so they can't."

And it was as simple as that, this one thought was the striking revelation that made Daniel decide to take his own life. It was so simple, so much so that he could not believe he hadn't thought of it sooner. The unthinkable had now become common sense.

Daniel was a logical person, perfectly suited to his newly ex-job as a data analyst. His first port of call was the computer, if he was going to do this, he was going to do it right.

He fired up his Powerbook and opened his Internet browser. With Google as his homepage he was just a few keystrokes away from all the answers he needed. He keyed in "suicide" and struck the enter key with a bizarre enthusiasm.

Within less than a second Google had returned its usual wealth of results, he clicked purposefully on the first link without even reading the summary.

In front of him opened a page with the heading "So you're thinking of committing suicide?" The page was a plea to any suicidal would be who may be looking to be talked round. It was full of extremely cotton wool-wrapped phrases about how every single soul is vitally important and you should be proud to be blessed with the one you have. The overall remit of the page was to keep you reading, in the vain hope that suicide was just a passing notion to you and that by the time you had read for a while you would have changed your mind.

"Is this it?" Daniel thought out loud. "Is this humanity's last sugar-coated attempt to cover up the fact that the whole world is just as fucked up as I am?" He decided not to waste anymore of his time with this site, he was here for advice on how to do it, not how not to. He closed the tab and returned to his search result.

The next page was much more promising, a forum dedicated to people talking about ways in which they fantasize about or are going to kill themselves. Daniel knew that statistically speaking most of this site would be worthless, but if you put enough crackpots in one place you're sure to get the odd idea that's just so crazy it might work.

His initial reading was disappointing, mostly just a bunch of hormonal teens complaining about how they're going to do "a shitload of pills" because "this guy from sixth form won't get off with me". Daniel caught himself wondering if he was that pathetic in his youth.

One thing that did stick out though was that each page had at least one reference to someone called "Jez" with posts like

"Why not call Jez" or "Give Jez a call, he'll know exactly what to do".

Daniel was still pondering over this when he came across the following post:

12/2/2008 – CrazyB17ch86 wrote:
Seriously you're all a bunch of sick idiots, but if I was going to kill myself then I'd just burn my house down. I got caught in a house fire when my parents got divorced and my dad was moving his shit out. I don't know how it started cause my parents both tell different versions, some sort of power trip or whatever. Anyway, I was in my room when it happened and all I remember is my room filling up with smoke and then waking up in the hospital. I guess my dad had run in to save my life or something. The point is I was talking to one of the orderlies at the hospital and he was telling me that in most fires it's not the actual fire that ever kills anyone but the smoke inhalation. Seriously, I don't even remember it, but if I hadn't been pulled out then I would have died for sure and I would have basically slept through the whole thing. Now I'll leave all you whiney little kids to go take some paracetamol or whatever. Beth

That's it! he thought. This is definitely the way to go. He wanted a way out, but a part of him still thought of his parents and the rest of his family. For what little he still cared about them he would rather be remembered as a guy who died in a terrible accident than the guy who killed himself. No matter how he sliced it this was the best solution. Now he just had to think of a plan that would cause a big enough fire that he could pass out from the fumes AND make it simultaneously look like an accident.

He had another mini revelation – people die all the time falling asleep whilst smoking, that would be an easy enough way to fake it. He had never smoked a day in his life mind you, but his parents didn't know that, often people turn to smoking or drinking as a coping mechanism in stressful times and let's face it, he'd been through his fair share of those. In fact as luck would have it he even knew where to find half a pack of cigarettes without even leaving the house.

Rachel had never been planned and up until the day they found out they were expecting her Izzy had been a smoker, albeit an extremely infrequent one. On the day she had done that pregnancy test and it had come out positive she threw the pack she kept on the bedside table into her wardrobe and there they had sat ever since.

Daniel ran into the room and foraged for them, holding them triumphantly in the air as if he had found some long lost artefact. He thought long and hard about the rest of the plan, moved a few things around in the room to "help the fire along" and retrieved the fire lighter from the drawer in the kitchen.

He got into bed and clutched the photograph one last time. He decided if it was found on the bed next to him it would look suspiciously like a suicide, so he placed it on the bedside table instead. He kissed the tips of his index and middle finger then spread them out so they were touching the lips of his wife and child.

"Goodnight, ladies, I'll see you in the morning."

He placed the cigarette in his mouth, sparked up the lighter and lit the tip. He had to take a long drag to get the thing going and this caused him to cough heavily. He never did understand why Izzy smoked these damn things.

He took one more long drag to get the cigarette burning nicely, coughed up some more and then let his hand drop to the side of the bed, the cigarette falling neatly onto a stack of work papers and bills he had strewn over the floor.

He remembered playing domino rally as a kid, how he would spend hours setting up the dominoes all over his room, the excitement building with each one placed, all leading up to that wondrous moment when you pushed over the first domino and set about an unstoppable chain of events. He remembered the disappointment he would get if after careful planning he had misplaced just one of the dominoes in the middle and the whole spectacle would come to an abrupt anti-climax. He closed his eyes and silently prayed this would not happen here, all he wanted was to be with his wife and child once more, wherever they were.

When he opened his eyes the fire had spread from the papers onto the rug. The rug ran all the way to the curtains, all highly flammable materials. He watched the fire spreading out, like the falling dominoes sweeping through the room. But instead of those black and white tiles the scene was set with dancing red and orange flames.

It was about this time he started to taste the smoke. Such an awful taste, like someone had shoved ten cigarettes in his mouth all at once, set them alight with a blowtorch and told him to chew.

He began to cough, only a few times at first, not enough to get him out of the bed. Then he coughed some more, stronger and more intense than before. Suddenly he could feel his determination to go through with it slipping through his fingers. Now he was coughing almost constantly and each one was like a shotgun blast to the chest.

He rallied all the last drops of fresh air in his lungs and made a daring attempt to get out. He could feel the heat from the fire now pulsing through the room, robbing it of all atmosphere. He could hear it crackling away violently like an army of children snapping twigs in autumn. The curtains were all but incinerated and the fire was spreading towards the doorway.

He knew this was his only shot but before he could make it barely two steps from his bed he dropped to his knees. He felt like it was his lungs that were on fire, not his bedroom. He desperately tried to crawl for the door but could make no ground. He had expended all the air he had and without its life giving properties his body simply refused to respond.

This was it, he thought, game over. All that was left to do was give in. With his final drop of energy he raised up his left hand as high as he could, saluting to the heavens which he hoped would await him.

And then blackness.

5

Before he opened his eyes he was already aware that he was someplace else. The sounds were distant and difficult to place as if he were underwater. He could hear a lot of talking but only the occasional word was discernable. It all had a very muted quality to it.

He tried to focus on a single sound and managed to find a dull repeating tone, it was happening every couple of seconds and it was getting louder, whatever it was it was getting closer.

Daniel soon realized that it was actually him that was getting closer, not the sound, and that he was doing this not by moving anywhere, but by waking up.

"Waking up?" he thought. "But... I'm not supposed to wake up!"

The beeping sound became more and more pronounced and Daniel soon realized it was the sound of a heart monitor. A machine that was letting him, and those around him know the one thing he didn't want to know – he was still alive.

He chanced to open his eyes, slowly at first, just a slit and then as they adjusted to the clinical white hospital lights wider and wider until things gradually started to come into focus.

He decided it was best to play dumb, one of the other pieces of information he had gleaned from the suicide forum was that if you were presented at A&E as a suspected suicide you would be forcibly placed under either hospital or home care for no less than 72 hours – for your own safety of course.

There was a nurse checking things around the bed and she smiled at him when she saw his eyes were open.

"Whe, where... am... I?" he said feebly.

"You're in the hospital Mr," she hesitated, "Brady." Clearly she had only just started her shift and was trying to cram all the patient names into her memory. Daniel appreciated the effort.

"The hospital?" he exclaimed. "What the hell am I doing here?"

"Well the doctor will be coming soon, Mr Brady, but basically you are here under observation for smoke inhalation, you were caught in a fire at your house and were brought in by paramedics about an hour ago."

She smiled again sweetly and excused herself, stating once more that the doctor would be with him shortly.

Paramedics? he thought, how the hell did they get there in time?

He didn't have time to ponder over this as the doctor truly was with him shortly, two of them to be exact. He felt honoured. The taller of the two doctors addressed him immediately.

"Hello, Mr Brady, I am Dr Miller and this is Dr Santiago." The shorter doctor gave a courteous nod and Daniel gave a smile back.

"First off I have to state how extremely lucky you were tonight…"

Daniel let out a little cough, he thought that had he been lucky then he wouldn't be here to have this conversation.

"And also," he continued, "how very stupid. Do you not know the perils of smoking in bed? I sincerely hope you have learned something from all of this."

Do the job properly next time? he thought sarcastically.

"All that being said," he continued, "the initial test results are back and so far they are much more positive than expected." This sounded promising. "However we would like to keep you in for a little while longer, just for observation."

"How much longer?" Daniel enquired.

"Well ideally overnight, just to be sure there are no complications. You were in a very serious accident tonight and we are unable to know the full extent of the damage at this time."

"Not an option," he snapped. "Is this *required*?" Daniel was still determined to finish the job and knew that he would not be able to do this with so many doctors around.

"No, sir, you are free to leave whenever you want, however we would always advise you to stay, just to get the all clear."

This level of concern sounded false and Daniel could see past the veneer to the fact that really the doctor would just like a quiet night. That must have been why he brought another doctor with him, so he could prove at a later date that Daniel had acted against the doctor's advice, should anything go wrong.

This suited Daniel down to the ground as no way was he staying the night in a hospital. Of course, he couldn't go home either, but he would figure something out.

He confirmed to Doctor Miller that he would like to leave and the two doctors promptly set off to have someone prepare the release papers.

When the nurse returned with his papers he stopped her to ask a question.

"Just one thing, how did I get here?"

"Like I said, Mr Brady, you were brought in by paramedics an hour ago."

"Yeah, but who called them?"

"I don't know exactly, the paramedics met the firemen at the scene and they worked together to get you out. I'm afraid that's all I know."

He thanked her and signed the forms. She handed him an appointment card for a follow up with the specialist the following Wednesday and wished him well.

"Actually, Mr Brady, just one more thing."

What could it be now? He just wanted to be out, but he thought if he just dealt with whatever little question she had it would allow him to get away quicker than simply fleeing the scene and drawing more undue attention. He turned back to face her.

"Yes?"

"We need you to update your next of kin information. We were unable to contact anyone on the number we have on record. A number of 07749…"

He didn't need to hear the rest, he knew it by heart, it was Izzy's mobile. He cut her off before she finished and gave her a false number he had just plucked from the air which seemed to satisfy her and he went on his way.

As he headed for the exit he cursed himself for surviving and was already thinking of ways to do the job properly. All being said though, the evening had taken its toll on him. He knew in his current state he would not be able to plan the smallest of things, let alone this. It would have to wait until tomorrow, tonight he needed to get himself to a hotel and get some sleep.

He was glad that the hospital hadn't deemed it necessary to change him into a gown. He was also glad he hadn't undressed when he got home from work as he still had his jacket with his wallet, phone and keys securely in the pockets. He had no signal on his phone so he headed to find the free phone to call a taxi when he heard a voice from behind him.

"Another attempted suicide eh?" The voice was seriously weathered and its presence was unexpected in a half empty hospital at this time of night.

"I don't know what you're talking about." Daniel responded without even turning to see whom he was talking to.

"Bullshit," the stranger spat. "I see your kind in here all the time. Want the easy way out, but when they realize the easy way is actually quite difficult, well then they invariably chicken out, screw it up and wind up here. You're lucky they haven't shipped you over to the crisis team for suicide watch, you must have made it look like a *real convincing accident.*"

This got Dan's attention. "Oh yeah? And what the hell would you know about it?"

"Let's just put it this way... does the name Jez mean anything to you?"

It took a moment for Daniel to put this piece of the puzzle in its place, then the penny dropped – that was the name of the mystery guy who kept cropping up on the forum. Suddenly the stranger had his full attention, Daniel turned to face him.

The guy was nothing unusual to look at, wearing a pair of faded jeans and a t-shirt under a jacket that was a colour that could only be described as "dirty brown". Short brown hair and no distinguishing facial features. He was sat down but Daniel could tell he was not particularly tall or short and of average build. In fact other than his strange choice of hangout he was completely unremarkable in every way, the kind of guy you passed on the street every day without even a second glance.

Daniel gave a little snort. "So you're this Jez then?"

"No, Mr Brady, I'm not," the stranger replied, sounding a little impatient. "But I do work for him."

How the hell did he know my name? Daniel thought but decided to play it cool.

"Well it seems you know who I am; I think it would only be fair if you told me your name."

"Let's just say I'm one of Jez's... 'recruitment agents'."

"And who exactly is this Jez character?"

"The less you know about him the better, but suffice to say he is someone who can offer a service that you definitely require. If your searches on the Internet earlier this evening are anything to go by."

He knew his name and he knew what he had been doing on the computer behind closed doors. To say that Daniel was a little unsettled by this would be a vast understatement.

"You seem to know an awful lot about me, so how about you cut the cloak and dagger routine and just tell me what the hell this is all about."

"Daniel, may I call you Daniel?" He didn't wait for a response. "We know more about you than you probably know about yourself. I am telling you this as I want you to believe in the seriousness of what I am about to offer you, it is quite literally a once in a lifetime opportunity." The stranger let out a small laugh, seeming particularly amused by this last statement.

At this point Daniel thought he was about to hear more sugar-coated crap or even some cult religion nonsense. He thought back to the forum and remembered that though he was mentioned frequently on the site, no actual information on how Jez would "help" was actually given. Probably just a power hungry nut-job who preys on people when they are at their lowest and convinces them to come and join some sort of "salvation programme" or something. He decided the time had come to end this conversation and so he lifted the receiver on the taxi phone.

"Please, Daniel, five minutes of your time and if what I am offering does not interest you then you can go back to trying to kill yourself the hard way."

"Five minutes? I'll give you four, my time is short don't you know?" This was said with an uncharacteristic sneer, what's more he couldn't believe that he was already making offhand remarks about the whole thing. He placed the handset down and took a seat to the man's left.

Daniel was often good at looking at things from many different angles, but the details of this mysterious stranger's offer were beyond anything he had ever read in his sci-fi novels.

"Basically, Daniel we offer a service not too dissimilar from what you tried to do for yourself tonight."

Daniel stared at him in silence and waited for him to continue.

"In my line of work I see a lot of people like you, people down on their luck, the loss of a loved one, or worse, a child. Convinced that life does not go on after-the-fact, you try to take your own life. And like so many others before you, you screw it up royally.

"I've got to admit, Daniel, you were a clever one. You actually managed to make the whole thing look like an accident, well to the paramedics and the doctors at least. Tell me, did you hold on to some strange delusion that had you succeeded in your attempts that the truth would never have come out?"

The stranger didn't wait for Daniel to verbalise an answer, he didn't need to, it was written all over his face.

"Had you been successful then you would have been subjected to a much more thorough investigation than the carpet sweep job that has been done here tonight. It would have taken the police no time at all to get hold of your Internet history and then a quick Google search on suicide, suspiciously on the same night as your 'accidental death' would be all the evidence anyone ever needed to say this was no accident."

Daniel felt like he was getting a lecture and interjected. "You've had three minutes already, and you still haven't told me about this offer."

The stranger dropped the preamble. "Daniel, what I am offering is that I, or indeed Jez, will finish the job you started. In no uncertain terms if you choose to accept our offer then your demise shall be extremely 'successful'."

Daniel was shocked; this had to be some sort of sick joke. He searched the stranger's face, his eyes, his expression for any signal that this was a setup, but he could find not one.

As if reading his mind the stranger spoke up, "I can assure you, Daniel, this is no joke."

They sat in silence for what seemed like an eternity. Daniel's resolve to end his own life had still not been broken and somehow this seemed like exactly what he needed. His curiosity was piqued, the four minutes were up, but now the stranger had Daniel's full and undivided attention.

"So what are you offering?"

"I've just told you, we will end your life on your behalf." Daniel couldn't help but be shocked at how nonchalantly this sentence seemed to just slip out of the stranger's mouth.

"Yes but I mean specifically, what will happen?"

"Again, Daniel, the less you know the better. Let's just say that once we have agreed the terms then you and I will go our separate ways and never see each other again. Then at some point over the next seven days you will be paid a visit by Jez. You will not see him and even if you were to see him you would not even know that it is him. You will not have to fear the end, it will be quick, it will be painless and best of all there will be no way of tracing it back to being a suicide. In fact it isn't actually a suicide, as it will not actually be you taking your own life. You will just become another victim of one of life's "little accidents" and the world at large will not view you as a coward, but as an unlucky soul, cut off in his prime."

"How will I die?"

"Again it's best you do not know, but even if I wanted to tell you I would not be able to, my part in all of this is almost over and any further details I'm afraid I just do not have."

"You mentioned terms. What are those?"

"Obviously, Daniel we do not offer this service as we simply wish to help put you out of your misery. There has to be something in it for us, a fee for services rendered if you will."

"But I don't have anything to offer, I'm just a data analyst, or at least was until yesterday."

"Daniel, do you really see much point lying to me at this stage? I already told you earlier that we know all about you and that includes that little account that you have in Jersey, which started with your uncle's inheritance and which you have been topping up since before you were even married. What's in there now? Around £40,000 is it?"

Daniel was taken aback. "Something like that yeah," he muttered.

"I'd say it's about £41,759.46, give or take a few pence. My figures are a few hours old after all."

Who the hell was this man? And how did he get so much information?

"So what do you want? The whole damn thing?"

"We're not greedy people, Mr Brady, £30,000 would be more than fair, would you not say? Leaving you with just shy of twelve thousand pounds to play with for your last week on earth."

"Oh yeah and what the hell am I supposed to do with that?"

"That, Daniel, is up to you; give the whole lot to charity if you like."

"So how do I get this money to you? And won't anyone get suspicious that I emptied my account out the same week I was murdered?"

"We prefer not to use the term murder, Daniel, think of it rather as a form of euthanasia. As for payment I have already left a briefcase in the boot of your car and will be returning for it tomorrow at 5 p.m. If the briefcase is empty then I shall assume that you have changed your mind, if it is full then we shall go ahead with our proposal. Either way you will not see me again. With regards to your cover story concerning the money, I have taken the liberty to arrange an appointment for you tomorrow morning with the travel agency on the high street near your old office. At eleven o'clock you will meet with John Swift who will have prepared an itinerary for a world cruise for you. You will of course accept at which point he will ask you for a deposit which you will pay by card, you will then ask him if it will be possible for you to pay the remainder of the cost in cash. If at any point he comments that you sound different on the phone you should merely state that you get told that often."

"It sounds like you guys have gone to a whole lot of trouble, planning every single detail like this."

"Mr Brady, I'm sure you can agree that is just as important for us as it is for you that none of what we discussed here tonight ever comes out. In fact you could say it is even more important for us, as you would not be around to face the consequences. I apologise for my candour," he added, "but in this line of work I have to keep it strictly business."

The stranger got up to leave and then glanced down at Daniel. "Any further questions?"

Daniel lowered his head towards his lap and silently shook it from side to side; he was still in a state of mild disbelief at what had just transpired. The man simply nodded and headed for the door. Daniel waited a moment to catch his breath before picking up the receiver and ordering a taxi. The operator informed him it would be ten minutes. He found a bench outside the entrance and waited.

6

True to their word the taxi arrived ten minutes later. Daniel got in and asked the driver to take him to the nearest hotel via a cash machine.

On the way Daniel spent his time gazing out of the window and thinking about everything that had just happened. Despite being sorely tempted by the stranger's offer he had yet to make up his mind. They pulled up at the cash machine; Daniel got out, drew £40 and returned to the car. A moment later they were on their way again.

No more than a few minutes later they arrived outside a building that Daniel didn't recognize. A sign outside read "Lucky Star" with another sign tied to the post below that read "Amazing value, rooms from only £18". This caused a serious question on the quality of the accommodation but he only needed it for one night so he paid the taxi driver and headed inside.

The reception area was what you would expect based on the sign outside, to describe it as a shithole would be flattery. There were two chairs in serious need of reupholstering on the left and a cobbled together desk area on the right behind which a girl, ostensibly in her late teens was busy "multitasking" in that she was simultaneously sleeping and chewing bubble gum.

"Excuse me!" Daniel said deliberately more loud than was necessary. "Can I get a room please?"

The girl practically fell straight off her chair but tried to casually sit up straight and spring to attention.

"Yes of course, sir, just give me one moment." She tapped away on the keyboard in front of her. "We only have twin rooms left right now, would that be OK for you?"

"Yeah, sure, whatever." He was usually full of manners but the effects of the night had left him weary and he had no time for formalities and even less patience. He needed a good night's sleep; that was the only way he could tackle his dilemma with a clear mind in the morning.

"Would you like breakfast, sir, or just the room?"

Daniel glanced around, with a reception area as insalubrious as this it begged the question of what the kitchen would be like and whatever he decided in the morning a case of salmonella was certainly not on the cards.

"Just the room thanks," he said and handed over his debit card. She hit a few more keys on the computer and clicked the mouse a few times, then leaned back in her chair to grab a key from the pigeonholes behind her. She took his payment and handed back his debit card along with the key.

"Room 407, it's on the 4th floor. The lift's out so you'll have to take the stairs."

This last piece of information was no surprise to Daniel; he nodded, turned and headed for the stairs, glad he didn't have any bags to carry. As he got up to the third floor he saw that the fire door had been broken off its hinges and he could hear what he assumed was a couple having an argument, mostly comprising of just screamed expletives. Daniel wondered how he had ended up in such a dive but carried on to his room regardless.

He opened the door after some serious issues with the lock and fumbled for the light switch. He found it and flicked it on abruptly. Of the three lights on the wall of the room only two of them were working and one of those was flickering erratically. He took off his jacket and hung it over the chair, kicked his shoes off and jumped on the bed still clothed. He decided he didn't want to get under these covers and that it would be prudent to sleep without undressing.

His head was spinning round, throbbing with a sensory overload. He lay on his back, folded his hands on his chest and took a large breath. He expected his thoughts to keep him up for the majority of the night, but surprisingly as soon as he closed his eyes he was asleep.

That night he dreamed of being on a far away island; he could feel the breeze on his face and hear the waves crashing against the shore. Beneath his feet was a beach of golden sand set to the backdrop of a lush, verdant forest. In the distance he saw a white horse galloping majestically along the shoreline. As the horse approached he could see a woman riding it, she had long flowing red hair but he could not make out any of her facial features. The horse galloped past him and came to a stop a few feet from where he was standing. The woman glanced over her shoulder, revealing a side profile of her face but still not enough for Daniel to catch any details.

"Are you not coming too?" she said, her voice echoing on as she continued to ride off into the distance.

And then he woke up.

7

A harsh blast of sunlight was streaming unforgivingly through the window; he hadn't even bothered with the curtains the night before. Not that it would have made much difference, he thought, the curtains were these paper thin, greyish things that stood little chance of holding off any of sunlight's brutal attack.

Daniel squinted and tried to sit up. He fell back down and began to cough. It felt like there was something on his chest that needed to break. He was coughing and spluttering for what seemed like minutes until finally he felt an ashy taste in his mouth. He ran to the bathroom and spat in the sink. The contents of his mouth looked like a thick soup of phlegm and tar, with just a touch of blood. "Nice," he thought and then turned on the tap.

The water spluttered to life and was more spat at him than a constant flow. Even the process of doing this caused the pipes to groan; he had to get out of this dive and fast.

He cleared the sink and then splashed some water on his face, trying to speed up the process of waking. Right then something suddenly hit him, what was the time? He checked his watch and saw that it was a little after ten. He couldn't believe it. This was the first time in the nearly seven years since the accident that he hadn't started the day with his strange ritual. The first day even that he has woken up anywhere other than at home. Something else hits him this morning, but it's not the sledgehammer he is used to. It's relief, clarity, serenity even as if the decision he needed to make the night before was sat there decided already, like a gift, wrapped and decorated with ribbons waiting to be opened.

He knew what had to be done. He was going to take the offer and be with his girls once more. No more need to think it through.

He returned to the main room and retrieved his shoes. He sat on the bed to pull them on and then completed the process by throwing on his jacket. He left the room hoping to never see it or another one like it ever again.

He descended to the reception area and was just about to put the key in the drop box and leave when he realized he had no idea where he was. He dropped the key in and got the attention of the receptionist, another teenager but this time a young man with a serious case of acne who was listening to music through a pair of headphones. Daniel had to wave his arms frantically to get his attention.

The guy lowered his headphones down to around his neck and cocked his head back to indicate Daniel had his attention. He confirmed this with some sort of grunt.

"Sorry to bother you," Daniel said sarcastically, "but where exactly are we?"

"We're in the Lucky Star, man," he said in an accent that suggested this kid spent most of his time watching movies involving Californian surfers.

"Yes, but on what road?"

"Oh, yeah, OK. We're on Ellington Road."

"Thanks, you've been very helpful," said Daniel with a wry smile.

He went outside and took out his mobile phone to call a taxi. He was running low on battery and had an unread text message from Johnnie that read:

"Maaaaaate." Daniel was not surprised to see he spelled his messages just like he talked. "What the hell went down in the office yesterday? It's all anyone's been talking about! I hope you're doing OK, man. Anyway, I'm going to this mental party on Thursday night so if you need something to do to take your mind off shit then gimme a bell yeah?"

He thought about deleting the message but then changed his mind. What else was he supposed to do with his last week on earth? Watch Battlestar Galactica reruns in his underwear? He called a taxi and waited for it to arrive.

As the taxi pulled up he had another quick glance at his watch, 10:26. Daniel knew what he needed to do. He told the taxi driver to take him to the high street, he had an eleven o'clock appointment to make at the travel agency. The journey took around fifteen minutes, he was twenty minutes early, not even enough time to go and get changed, so he decided to just get this part of the process over and done with. He entered into the agency and started reading the little name wedges on the desks.

"Excuse me, sir," came a call from across the office, "can I help you at all?"

"Yes, I'm looking for John Swift."

"Well that's me, and you are?"

"Daniel Brady. I'm sorry I'm a little early for my appointment."

"Mr Brady, of course." Swift looked him up and down, Daniel detected a hint of disbelief in the man's face, probably to do with the fact that Daniel was stood there in the clothes from the fire most likely looking like he'd just been dragged through a burning bush; and yet he was expected to believe that this man was interested in booking a world cruise. "I'm sorry, sir, from your voice on the phone I expected someone a little... older," he concluded diplomatically.

"Yeah I get that a lot," Daniel replied right on cue.

"I'll bet. Please take a seat, sir, based on what you said over the phone I took the liberty of preparing an itinerary on your behalf. It's right here at my desk." The look on his face suggested that he was in need of some praise for all of his hard work. He was quite young after all and Daniel thought this would have been quite a big deal for Swift.

"Wow, it seems like you've been working hard on this, thank you," Daniel said half-genuinely, Swift smiled back, beaming with pride.

He took a seat in front of Swift's desk which was extremely well organized, the only clutter being a half full coffee mug and a framed photograph which Daniel could only get a side profile on. Even the itinerary was stored neatly in a draw, out of sight.

"You're going to love the package we have put together for you. The cruise line we have chosen have just opened this new long stay service where you do a traditional world cruise, however you remain at each of the destinations for up to 5 nights. Really allowing you to get a true feel for each of the places you will be visiting. Of course we will sort out all of your visa documentation in advance so you'll be able to sail through customs, sorry, no pun intended. There is of course the painful part…"

"OK, how much is it?"

"No, sir, not the cost, I was referring to the inoculations you will require," he said with a nervous laugh. Daniel gave an encouraging smile back as he could see Swift had been working on that joke. "These are all detailed in appendix B of your itinerary and if you could arrange these with your GP soon then that will make things run smoothly. Now, would you like me to go through the locations with you?"

"No that's OK, just let me know how much of a deposit you require, I'm happy to go ahead with everything."

"Oh!" Swift said with a look of complete shock. "Well, if you're sure, sir. Well we need a deposit of £500 today, sir to secure your place. The remainder of the payment can be made in instalments, providing that the full sum has been paid at least a month before departure."

"Actually, I would like to pay the full sum off next week, is it possible to pay by cash?"

"Of course, sir, but with such a large amount would you not feel more comfortable doing it electronically?"

"No it's not a problem. My bank is right here on the high street, I'm sure it will be safe enough."

"Ok then, sir, how would you to pay your deposit?"

"Credit card."

"OK, I'll just go fetch the machine."

Swift scurried off excitedly towards the back of the office, suddenly Daniel had a thought, the money in his account, it was in Jersey, not his local bank, how was he going to get hold of it so soon?

Swift returned with the card reader and took the payment. Everything went through quick and painless. Daniel started to rise from his chair when his card was returned to him and Swift followed. "If you have any further questions…" he said, extending his hand out towards Daniel, "please don't hesitate to get in touch, or just pop in anytime. You have my number right?"

Daniel shook the young man's hand with his right hand as he was handed the itinerary in a glossy A4 folder to his left. Daniel nodded and they exchanged a polite smile before Daniel exited the building.

As soon as he was outside he got out his phone and located the number for his banker in Jersey. He had to key in his account number, date of birth and security code before the phone connected to an operator.

"Good morning, Mr Brady, how may we help you today?" The geek inside Daniel was impressed that the telephone system had called up his details ready for the banker; he loved little automated touches like that, even down to when the local pizza place installed a phone recognition system and would greet him by name, knowing his regular order.

"Yes, hello, I was wanting to close my account and transfer my balance to my current account here in England."

"Of course, Mr Brady, but may I first ask why you are wishing to close your account? Are there any issues we could possibly help you with?"

"No, I don't have any problems with the service, I am just planning on taking a world cruise and need the funds where I can access them more directly."

"Oh how lovely, Mr Brady. Well I will get on to that straight away for you so you can start planning your trip. Can you just confirm the details of the account you wish to transfer the funds to?"

"Yes, you will have it on records already, it's where the monthly instalment comes from."

"Would that be the account ending 3907?"

"Yes that's the one."

"OK fantastic, I can put that transfer through for you now and it should be cleared within your other account within the next 3 days. Your account here will remain open for now however as we require written confirmation before cancelling any account. It will effectively be frozen though so there will be no outstanding transactions for you to worry about."

"Three days?" Daniel said as his heart sank almost to his stomach. "Is there no way it can be done any quicker?"

"Well we do offer an immediate service, which depending on your bank could be cleared within the hour. There is however a charge for this service."

Daniel couldn't care less about the charge right now, he just didn't want to miss this "opportunity". "How much?"

"1% of the overall sum transferred, so for this it would be £417.59, would that be OK?"

Daniel's memory flashed back to the night before, that slick bastard had been right to the last pound, he didn't know whether to be impressed or disturbed. "Yes that would be fine," he confirmed without a moment's second thought.

"OK, I just need to reconfirm your date of birth and security code to complete the transfer."

He gave her these two pieces of information. "It looks like congratulations are in order," she said.

"I'm sorry?"

"It was your birthday yesterday, happy belated birthday Mr Brady."

He managed a mumbled thanks while he could hear her clicking away on the computer down the phone line.

"Ok, sir, that's all done, is there anything else I can help you with today?"

"No, thank you, that will be all."

"OK, well thank you for your custom over the years and on behalf of the whole company I would like to wish you a very safe and enjoyable trip."

"Thank you," he said and he put down the phone. He had at least an hour before the money would be cleared at the bank so he thought it was about time he went home for a change of clothes, to charge his phone and to survey the damage.

8

As he turned the corner into his street he held his breath as his house came into view; he was expecting the worst. The situation however wasn't that bad, all things considered. His bedroom window had been blown out; presumably by the heat, and all around where the frame had been were black scorch marks. The debris from his window lay strewn about, obviously the fire department's prime concern was to stop the fire and the rest was up to you. He found some slight comfort in knowing he would never have to go through the hassle of dealing with it though. That didn't make the scene any less unsettling however. He approached the house and prepared himself for what the interior might have in store.

As he entered the house there was a stench of smoke in the air, so thick it was almost palpable. He wafted his hand in front of his face in a futile attempt to clear the atmosphere. This did absolutely nothing and the ashen residue had already started giving his lungs hell. Whatever he needed to do in the house it was clear that he should do it fast.

He headed up the stairs to a small landing from which he could see all of the four rooms on the first floor. From this vantage point he could see that the extent of the fire damage was much more obvious inside the house. The door to his bedroom was pretty much incinerated and the charred outline that he had seen on the window from outside was here too, but this time much more widespread and pronounced. He could see the room within, a blackened mess, his bed a charcoal husk sat ghostlike in the middle of the room. He decided that checking the wardrobes for clean clothes would be a worthless enterprise; thankfully he knew there was some clean washing yet to be sorted in the utility room.

He headed downstairs and through the combined dining area and kitchen which sat below his bedroom. There was a substantial amount of water damage, seemingly from the fire brigade's efforts to stop the blaze. A large patch of sodden plasterboard on the ceiling was still dripping water onto the dining table below and looked like it could give way at any point.

The utility room was a small compartment off the side of the kitchen and was barely large enough to fit the combination washer/dryer which it housed. On the counter above sat a washing basket full of clean clothes. Daniel grabbed a pair of jeans, some underwear and a few tops. He went out into the hallway and rummaged sloppily under the stairs for his old gym bag. He found it at the back underneath the tent he had never used and the cushions for the garden furniture.

He stuffed the extra tops into the bag and got changed right there in the hall, leaving the clothes of the day before exactly where they fell. Daniel had always been a bit of a neat freak and instead of making him uneasy this new reckless abandon was actually extremely liberating, even if clothes on the floor would only be a minor crime to most. Thinking ahead he collected together his passport and a handful of utility bills, he didn't want to be caught short if the bank asked him for proof of his identity.

He grabbed the bag, picked up a phone charger that was plugged in near the front door and headed outside desperate to be back in the fresh air. Sat there was his old Golf; it was red once but the years, the miles and the sun had seen fit to turn it this sort of salmon colour. He didn't even know if the old thing still ran. After the accident he had stopped driving altogether. Izzy had been driving a supposedly safety award winning 4x4, so that didn't exactly leave him with much confidence for his old banger.

He went over to the car and tried to open the boot which to his surprise was still locked. His heart sank. He knew it, the entire encounter the previous night hat been a hoax. That can't be it, he thought but some faint glint of curiosity led him to take out his keys and unlock the car. He opened the boot and there it was, sat smack bang in the middle, a silver attaché case which looked like it had never even been opened. Daniel couldn't help but smirk at how surreal the whole situation was. Had there been some dry ice causing a mist around the case it would have been something straight out of a movie. He supposed though that he should not be surprised that the man, whoever he is could open a locked boot, after all he did seem to know everything else about him. Sheepishly he looked over each shoulder before taking out the case. He slammed the boot shut.

As the boot closed he was startled to find someone standing right next to the car. It was Mrs Bridge from across the street.

"Daniel, oh my gosh, I'm so glad to see that you're OK."

He smiled politely. "Yeah, nothing to worry about; doctors gave me the all clear this morning."

"I was just so worried last night when the ambulance and the fire engine turned up, I didn't know what was going on, then I looked up to your window and could see the flames, I feared the worst, Daniel, I thought…"

She trailed off into a small cry. She was pushing 90 by Daniel's best guess and she had never really held down a full conversation with him without going off on some wild historical tangent.

"Well look," he said in a reassuring tone, "I'm all good and see," he pumped his fist twice on his chest and had to disguise the fact that he had almost caused another coughing fit, "I'm fit as a fiddle. Now how about I help you back home and pop the kettle on for you? How's that sound?"

She sniffed and regained some of her composure. "No, you're OK, young man, I can make it on my own, there's life in the old girl yet!"

"Just one more thing," he said as she was preparing to walk away, "so, it wasn't you who called the ambulance?"

"No, dear, like I said the first thing I saw was when the emergency vehicles turned up."

"Did you see anything else? Maybe earlier in the day?"

"No, nothing that I can think of, last thing I saw was you opening the back of your car, around the time I was closing my curtains."

"But I…" He decided to stop there, the old lady's eyesight wasn't great anymore and he realized almost immediately that what she had seen was in fact the stranger and not him. He thought it best to leave her thinking that, just in case at some point next week she was given the same line of questioning he had just administered by the police. "OK, Mrs Bridge, thanks for your help anyway."

"Anytime, dear. Do you need anywhere to stay? My spare room probably isn't what you youngsters are used to but you're more than welcome to it while you get back on your feet."

"Thank you for the offer, but I have already made other arrangements." A little white lie, but he didn't want her to insist or be offended.

"Alright, suit yourself, you take care of yourself now, young man."

"I will and you too."

"Oh you can count on that!" And with that she was tottering off back to her house. Daniel couldn't for the life of him comprehend how she had got the jump on him when she moves at a snail's pace. With the case in hand he headed back to the high street.

9

He arrived at the bank shortly after midday. It was manned by a skeleton crew suggesting the majority of the staff had already left for lunch. He walked up to the first counter, sort of a concierge desk set in front of the main business area and explained that he had come to empty his account. The clerk informed him that he would need to speak with a manager and at present they were all busy. He instructed Daniel to take a seat in the waiting area and informed him that a manager would be with him as soon as possible.

As he sat and waited he thumbed through some of the various brochures that were on display. Pamphlets with inquisitive titles such as "Are you happy with your mortgage?" or "Is your personal savings account giving you the returns that you need?" He had always found the advertising through a question approach quite comical but today his mind was distracted by much more serious things. Like who the hell had called the ambulance?

A short while later a manager appeared. A rotund man with a beaming smile, who by the looks of things was in his early forties. He was wearing an Armani suit and had not a single hair out of place. Pfft, Daniel thought, poor economy my arse!

He was moving towards Daniel with a surprising amount of grace for such a large gentleman and he had his hand outstretched and ready for shaking.

"Mr Brady!" he said in a commanding tone. "Sorry to keep you waiting, please follow me to my office."

By office he meant cubicle, a 2mx2m square made out of partitions that barely reached a quarter of the way to the top of the bank's vast Edwardian interior. More of the brochures from outside were fanned out neatly on one side of his desk.

"So," he began, "how may I help you today?"

Daniel noted his use of the word "I" as opposed to the telephone banker earlier using "we"; clearly this guy believed he WAS the bank!

"Yes, I'm here to close my current account please."

"That's a terrible shame, Mr Brady, is there any reason for this? I would greatly like to discuss any problems you may have and see if they can't be resolved."

He went through a similar dialogue with him as the previous banker about having no problems and just needing the cash for a trip he had planned. This may have worked earlier, but it seemed this guy was much more reluctant to lose a "valuable customer".

"Well, Mr Brady, have you considered there are many ways in which we could help make this experience much more secure and hassle free for you? We could change the limit on your cards for example or even order any foreign currency you need?"

Daniel was determined not to be pushed around here and so he called on all of his reserves of bravado. "No," he said in an authoritative tone. "I have already considered my options and I am 100% certain on how I would like to handle my affairs. If you look at my account you will see I have already made a substantial transaction today in preparation for this. Now if you please I would like you to close my account and get me my money, thank you."

The manager was aghast. "Yes, Mr Brady, of course." He repositioned himself in his chair before continuing to speak. "Could you please give me your account information and may I see either your driver's license or your passport?"

Daniel handed over his passport and debit card which had all the required information.

The manager, who by this time Daniel had found out was called Mr Staker – how very apt, a cold piece of wood that could kill even a vampire – typed away on his keyboard. After a moment or so his face dropped into a concerned frown and he reached for his phone.

"Everything OK?" Daniel enquired.

"Yes, yes, just a little something I need to double check that's all, nothing to worry about." Something in those last four words sounded all too familiar.

Staker talked away discretely on the phone, most of it was inaudible to Daniel but he got the general gist that he was talking to someone further up the food chain. His pompous demeanour would show no weakness. A moment later he placed the phone back down and returned his attention to Daniel.

"OK," he started. "I can give you your money today but unfortunately I will not be able to close your account without your wife's signature."

Daniel was incredulous, how can it be so easy to move all of the money around but so difficult to close an account? Surely the money was the important part? "That's not going to be possible," he said with an audible amount of contempt in his voice.

"OK, well you can either have her pop in at a time that is more convenient or you could write to us, whichever is easier for you."

"No, you don't understand. I don't mean that it's not possible today, I mean it's not possible ever. My wife was killed in a car accident seven years ago." By now he was fuming and fighting hard to stay in control.

"Oh, I'm so sorry, Mr Brady." Staker was clearly horrified at his faux pas. His sympathy didn't last however as he headed straight into the next tirade of red tape. "In that case, sir we will need to see a death certificate before we are able to close the account."

Daniel took as big a breath as he could manage before impatiently barking, "Whatever!" He had given up, he couldn't care less if the account was closed or not and if he argued any further he would be liable to give an encore of yesterday's Bruce Lee show. "I will bring it in another time. Now can we sort out the money today please?" This last pleasantry added more out of frustration than good manners.

"Of course, please just wait here a moment and I will go and retrieve the money from our vault." He got up and left Daniel alone with his thoughts.

Daniel attempted to process all the events of the last 24 hours. It had barely been a full day since this all started, with Framer and the guy in the suit pointing across the office and yet here he was, in the middle of something that he could never have even imagined. The order of everything seemed to blur into one right now, the hospital, the fire, Framer's office; they all seemed to happen in no particular order, in the same moment and yet simultaneously separated by years. Like memories thrown into a vat and mixed into one, he tried desperately to hold on to any single thought for more than a moment.

Then it came to him again, that dream of the woman on the beach. He had never been much of a dreamer and dubious of anyone who would try to analyze such things, yet here he was, early on a Tuesday afternoon lucidly dreaming without even falling asleep.

It was a dream but he was in control. He could see the whole thing, rewind it, pause it, slow it down, but his power stopped at seeing anything new, he could not catch her face no matter how hard he tried. He watched her ride away over and over, the desire to follow increasing with every repetition.

What does it all mean?

Where is this place?

Who *is she*?

Before any of the answers could come to him he was dragged abruptly back to reality by Staker's return. The large man was carrying an equally large bag; he was like the Santa Claus of the banking world. He placed the sack aside his chair and sat back down.

"OK, do you have any way of carrying all this?"

Daniel lifted up the case and tapped on it twice with his other hand. Staker gestured for him to place it on the desk. Daniel did so and opened it, Staker began placing the money in whilst counting out loud.

Daniel had only ever seen money like this written as a number on some paper or in a spreadsheet; seeing it in hard cash was a much different experience, blocks of £1000 all in fifties and wrapped in a seal bearing the bank's branding.

"1... 2... 3... 4..." Staker counted, the case devouring each brick as he went. Then a little while later. "38... 39... 40... 41." There was just the last few hundred to go in now. All that money and yet it barely filled the case. What had looked like so much only a moment ago seemed to shrink somehow once inside. This was it, everything he and Izzy had saved for, the holidays they never got to take, the restaurants they never got to eat at, the new sofa they were talking about getting once Rachel was a little older, all of it, reduced to a pile of notes sat mute within the case.

"Would you like me to count it again, sir?"

Daniel snapped back to reality. "No, it's OK, thank you."

He closed the case and rose to his feet, Staker stretched out his hand once more. "Well, Mr Brady, thank you for your business and I hope that you have a fantastic trip." He sounded decidedly less sincere than the woman earlier, Daniel thought, but then again you can be anything you want down the phone.

Daniel left the office and then left the bank, knowing exactly what was left to do but still bewildered all the same.

10

He found himself longing for some familiarity, he checked his watch and it was nearing one o'clock so he headed for JC's. Jeanie was there as always and she greeted him with a smile and a hearty hello. Daniel said hello back, excused himself and made a beeline for the bathroom.

He decided if nothing else, that there was no way he was leaving any more money than the £30,000. He had come to terms with the arrangement he had made with the stranger the night before but there was obviously still a certain degree of mistrust and more than a hint of aversion towards him. The cool way in which he had held himself made Daniel's skin crawl.

He opened his backpack and placed it on the floor. Then he placed the attaché case on the toilet seat and opened that also.

He furtively grabbed at eleven of the bricks, secreting each one in his backpack. Someone knocked on the door of the bathroom and he nervously bleated out, "Just a minute!" He quickly packed the rest of the change and returned to the main area.

"Going somewhere nice, dear?" This was Jeanie.

"I'm sorry?"

"The backpack and briefcase? You look like you're heading somewhere."

"Oh right, OK. No, I just had a few things to sort out, that's all." He didn't want to get into any unnecessary conversations about the fire, but he was surprised that in a town this small and with him living so close to the high street that news of his "accident" had not preceded him.

"Alright, so what can I get you?"

"Just the usual," he said but then reconsidered. "Actually, could I get two poached eggs on toast?"

"Feeling adventurous today are we? Take a seat and I'll bring them right over for you."

He picked a seat in the corner and sat diagonally with his back to the wall and window. Usually he would look out of the window and watch the world go by, but today he didn't feel like he needed the distraction. He watched as Jeanie pottered about on the stove before she dutifully came with some orange cordial, Daniel's drink of choice.

"No work today then?"

He was in a taciturn mood and only managed a simple grunt insinuating he had not fully understood her observation.

"Well you're very casually dressed, I just thought maybe you had the day off?"

"Yeah, I just decided to take a day to myself; as I said earlier I had a few things to sort out." He was careful to not come across as stand-offish, his mind was elsewhere but Jeanie deserved better than that.

"Oh we all need those days from time to time."

They exchanged a smile and she started for the counter, before she was barely two steps away she turned on her heels. "Oh, I forgot to ask you, that thing you were worrying over yesterday, did it ever happen?"

"No no, nothing to worry about." He gave a gentle smile in an attempt to disguise this last untruth.

"Glad to hear it, see, I told you these things always turn out right."

A few tables over there was a stack of magazines, originally stocked by Jeanie and then replenished over time by the addition and interchange of things customers had left behind. Daniel grabbed one off the pile and returned to his table. He flipped it over to see that he had landed upon a copy of *Gardeners World*. He would have preferred it to have been *New Scientist* but in all fairness he had no intention of actually reading it so for now garden gnomes were as good as genomes. He flicked through the pages, giving a superficial glance to the pictures while taking no mind whatsoever of any of the content.

Out of the corner of his eye he saw the door to the café swing open and a woman with a blonde bob walked in. She was wearing a long flowing dress – unseasonal for spring – and moved with grace. She approached the counter as if floating on air. Jeanie as she would with any other customer greeted her without a moment's hesitation.

"Can I help you, miss?"

"Yes actually, I was wondering if you could tell me where I could find a park nearby?" The woman spoke with an accent which Daniel did not recognize, he thought it may be Eastern European but any further localization was impossible.

"Oh dear, well I know where there is one, but I'm afraid I'm terrible with directions, but I think young Daniel here may be able to help you."

Daniel's ears pricked up at the sound of his name, he craned his neck to see what was being said. "What's that, sorry?"

"This young lady here needs directions to a park, I thought maybe you might be able to help her out?"

Daniel glanced around the room and was suddenly very aware that he was the only person there other than Jeanie and this new woman. Before he got a chance to respond she was already heading over to his table.

"Oh great," she said. "That would be fantastic, Daniel is it?"

Daniel was dumbstruck. "Errrrr, ummmmm, weeeeell."

"I'm Helena," she offered, extending her hand.

"Helena," he repeated giving her hand a quick shake.

"No He-lur-na," she said smiling and accenting the correct syllable. He repeated it once more attempting to copy how she had said it.

"Well, what sort of park are you looking for?"

"I don't mind, I just would like to take a walk, somewhere with trees where I can watch the first signs of spring." There was an ethereal and romantic tone to her voice, as if she had not a care in the world.

Daniel thought on, surveying the woman in front of him. "Well, we actually have a couple in the area."

She waited for a pause in his speech before briefly interrupting. "I'm sorry do you mind if I sit?"

Daniel gestured, palm up to the chair at the opposite side of the table, she took a seat and a moment later Jeanie placed his food in front of him. She asked if either of them would like anything else, Helena politely ordered a coffee.

"Go on, eat," she said to him, more of a gentle encouragement than an order.

"I would feel rude, eating in front of you like that."

"Don't be silly, please eat your lunch and you can tell me about the parks afterwards."

He did so with a childlike obedience; something about the way she talked had an enchanting nature to it. He felt like he would do anything this woman said. Occasionally he would look up from his plate and see her smiling at him. It should be unnerving having someone just watch you eat, he thought, however there was comfort in her gaze and warmth in her smile.

Jeanie delivered the coffee, Helena emptied two sachets of sugar into the cup and stirred it hypnotically. She gave the mug a gentle blow before taking a lingering and thoughtful sip. Daniel was entranced.

Her beauty was apparent, the blonde bob cut to follow the natural contours of her face, her eyes ice blue, her skin soft and radiant. Everything about her was beguiling, even her smell, a subtle breath of perfume reached out its fingers to him across the table and drew him in further. He ate his eggs and she sipped her coffee. He found himself doing this without even looking at his plate, their gazes inextricably locked.

When he was done he wiped his mouth politely and placed his napkin neatly down on the table.

"So," he continued, "as I was saying there are a couple in the area."

"Well which would you recommend?"

"Personally I like Elmwood Park, it's not very far from here, has a lot of greenery – although you'll be hard pushed finding that anywhere at this time of year – and there aren't many cyclists or runners clogging up all the paths. It even has a small duck pond."

Daniel was all set to continue with the descriptions of some other parks but Helena didn't allow him the chance. "Sounds lovely, and how do we get there?"

Daniel picked up on the use of the word "we" but chalked it off to Helena not speaking her primary language - whatever that was – so he decided to not give it a second thought.

"If you head out of here and cross the street you will see Rydal Road, it's the one opposite, between the chemist and the charity shop. Go down there until you get to the end and then turn left, that should be Albion Road. Then if you head down that road and take the third right onto Clapham Road that will take you straight there."

She repeated the directions back to him, her English was better than most actual English people he knew and he found her accent truly intoxicating. He thought back to the dream, the woman on the beach, but she had long flowing red hair and Helena had a blonde bob. He shouldn't hold on to such daydreams, he would probably never see this woman again in his life.

She finished her coffee in silence; the same welcoming smile on her face between sips. Every so often the left hand side of her lip would sneak up a little further than the rest of her smile; he was truly disarmed by her. In his mind he was rapidly formulating ways to extend their time together; he could ask some more questions, he could offer her another coffee, some food even, but before he could muster the words she was already rising to leave. She thanked him and headed for the door.

He felt as though something wondrous had been taken from him and his head began to drop to his chest. But right then at the last moment she turned and said five words that would go on to change everything:

"Are you not coming too?"

11

Daniel rose from his seat but it was as if the world had been enveloped in a mist. Time compressed and his senses were focused solely on this bewitching woman who stood before him. He fought desperately to control his mind; it was like an internal conversation had been sparked inside him between two different parts of his personality.

Is it the dream?

Don't be absurd!

But she said the same words…

Just a coincidence, she hasn't even got red hair!

Just a technicality… this is a sign….

You don't *believe* in signs

She *said the words!!!*

Enough about the words, fine, if you do this, you do it alone.

"Daniel?" This voice was real, it was Helena.

"Sorry?"

"Are you not coming too?"

By this point he had been abandoned of all rhyme and reason, she entranced him, but more importantly, he had nothing left to lose. "Sure, why not. But I just need to drop something off at my house first, it's on the way though." OK, so maybe not *all* rhyme and reason had left him.

Daniel made to pay for his food and asked for Helena's drink to be included in the bill but before Jeanie had a chance to speak Helena had already thrust a £20 note towards the café owner stating that it is the least she could do to thank Daniel for his tourist guide duties. Daniel being one of the last partisans that claim chivalry is alive and well objected profusely but his protests fell on deaf ears.

"I insist!" she said emphatically and she turned to leave without waiting for any change. Daniel followed, utterly ensnared.

They headed out of the café and Daniel took a tentative lead. "So, I noticed from you're accent you're not from round here, do you mind me asking where you are from?"

"I'm from Prague, in the Czech Republic," she said with a questioning tone in her voice as if making sure Daniel knew where that was.

"OK, I thought somewhere in Eastern Europe but couldn't put it any more specific."

"Well now you can," she said playfully. "Don't worry about it even people from home wouldn't be able to place it. My accent is a little mixed up as my parents are both from separate parts of the former Soviet Union. Then it's further confused by the fact that I travel a lot."

"So you're a big traveller then?"

"You could say that, I write for a travel magazine back home."

"That's fantastic; I bet you get to see some great places?"

"Well, yes and no, I do get to travel a lot, but I am always writing about it, and instead of just enjoying a particular place I'm always thinking of how to later put it into words. I'd much prefer to just be in the moment."

"So what brings you to our charming little town then? Surely the people of Prague aren't concerned with the goings on of a tiny suburb this far outside London?"

"I'm actually here on vacation, my first non-business trip to England as it happens."

"And you chose here? Why?"

"I think you get a better feel for the people and the country if you stay away from the big cities. People get so many stereotypes about places and I prefer to get past that and find the 'true' picture of a country."

"Well hopefully this town won't put you off coming back, nothing ever happens here. I'm surprised you haven't left already down to sheer boredom!"

"Don't be silly, I really like it here. Personally I find there is always something happening, you just need to look for it right. That's as true here as it would be in London or Paris or Rome."

Daniel thought on this for a moment as they made their way to his house. This town had always been dull, even when he was looking for excitement in his late teens. "OK, I just need to drop this at my car, this is it here."

She looked to the car and then to the house; it would be impossible not to notice the fire damage, in fact Daniel was surprised she hadn't done sooner. "Oh my gosh," she said with surprise. "What happened to your house?"

"Oh, nothing, just a little fire."

"It looks like a whole lot more than a *little* fire. How did that happen?"

"I was smoking in bed," he said sheepishly as she shot him a disapproving glare. "I know, I know, it was a very stupid thing, believe me I have *definitely* learned my lesson!"

"I'm just glad you're OK actually." There was sincerity in her voice that made him feel like he was talking to an old friend rather than an enigmatic stranger who had blazed into his life quicker than the flames of the night before.

He placed the case in the boot of the car, closed and locked it. He didn't see much point in leaving it unlocked, the stranger had got the case into a locked car, he would surely be able to get it out again. "Right, that's it, shall we get to this park then?"

As they walked they talked some more, Daniel found out that Helen's mother and father were from Latvia and Russia respectively but had settled in Prague when her mother was expecting. Daniel was full of questions but Helena was very proficient at returning the focus of the conversation to him.

"So what do you do for work?" she asked.

"Actually, I lost my job yesterday." He didn't know whether he was fired or he quit really, so "lost my job" seemed the most factually correct statement available at the time.

"Oh that's great news," she said excitedly.

Daniel was confused by this statement. "How do you figure that?"

"Well it means you can be my tour guide for a bit longer, doesn't it?"

It was a very presumptuous question that seemed to miss the core fact that Daniel had been recently dealt some very bad news, but there was something about the way her eyes lit up when she said this that was hard to argue with.

"I guess it does!" Daniel replied. He couldn't believe the words coming out of his mouth. It was as if in accepting that his end was coming he had ironically been given new life.

She gave an ingenuous clap before regaining her composure with a subtle cough.

When they reached the park the springtime sun was hanging low in the sky. The trees hadn't quite started to bud yet and if it wasn't for a very unseasonal clear blue sky it would feel more like winter than spring.

The smell in the air reminded him of walks through this very park he used to take with Izzy. He felt a sudden pang of guilt as if he were betraying her by being here with another woman. He told himself that he was just showing this new woman around and that there was nothing culpable about it. He felt though that this wasn't so much of a reminder, but more of a subtle deceit to appease his conscience.

"Oh, it's beautiful here." Helena interrupted his train of thought again; she was exceedingly good at doing that!

"Yeah, I used to come here with my wife and daughter." Why was he mentioning them? He never talked about them to anyone, not even his parents. So why was he talking about them to a complete stranger? Was it a by-product of the guilt? Maybe to honour their memory he was speaking about them, proving his loyalty?

"Oh," she said, her tone growing concerned. "You said used to? Where are they now?"

"They died... Nearly seven years ago."

"Oh my God, I'm so sorry." He had heard this a lot, everyone was always "so sorry" as if it was their fault in some way. But this was different. She was stood aghast with her hands cupped around her nose and mouth. Tears had already formed in the corners of her eyes. This wasn't mere fabricated sympathy, this was genuine grief.

"Hey, hey, it's OK," he said and before realizing it he had a single arm wrapped around her, squeezing her shoulder gently. She lifted her eyes to meet his. They were so indescribable;

unfathomably blue yet ice white at the same time. The glistening tears looked like they would freeze right there, like tiny glaciers. She stared back into his eyes and it was like she was staring through him. There was an unquestionable feeling of empathy, like the look in her eyes mirrored his pain in a tragically perfect way.

Daniel tried to grasp hold of this indefinable force. He thought back to his science books and all the theories within. How could he describe it?

Electricity?

Magnetism?

Gravity?

None of these words seemed to fit, there was definitely an energy here but not one that could be measured in joules or Newtons or watts. This was an energy that was measured in heartbeats, in breaths, in butterflies.

This moment seemed to stretch out before him but just as soon as it was happening it was all over. They broke their gaze and put some space between them, turning their bodies away shyly, like adolescents who had just discovered their first crush.

Daniel steeled himself. "Ahem, would you like to see the rest of the park?"

"That would be lovely."

They walked around the rest of the park in a strange silence as the sun set behind the trees. Every now and then he would risk a glance at her, most of the times he caught her looking back, a subtle yet warming smile fixed upon her lips. If only he could get back that moment.

12

They tacitly agreed it was time to leave just as the sun was low enough for the streetlights to come on. Neither of them had a destination in mind and the conversation which had been so free flowing moments earlier had now stagnated. Finally just as it seemed that the silence would endure indefinitely Helena spoke up.

"Do you have any plans for tonight?"

"Not really." He didn't know where this flaky answer came from, he had no plans. Perhaps he just wanted to see what she would say next without seeming like a loner.

"What does that mean?"

"OK, no, I don't have any plans."

"Do you like music?"

He gave this a brief thought, his music collection consisted mainly of the two classics: his classical collection of Brahms, Vivaldi and Gershwin which he would always listen to whilst studying in his youth – and the small selection of classic rock his dad had tried to "educate" him with: Zeppelin, The Stones and the like. He concluded that he probably would not be able to name any songs or artists that were popular at the moment or in fact from probably since he left university. He felt somewhat of a fraud but decided to answer in a non-committal but affirmative manner.

"Who doesn't?"

"Great, well there's this gig I'm going to tonight and I was wondering if you'd like to accompany me?"

"As long as by *accompany me* you mean join you in the crowd and not on stage then sure, I'm in."

"Yes, of course," she said giggling. "Although I would *love* to be on stage with these guys! But no, we will be there merely to watch."

She looked at her watch. "My gosh where has the time gone?" Daniel thought this would be the part where the small talk gets left there and for her to make a sharp exit. Thankfully this did not happen. "The doors open at 7:30, we'll need to go back to my hotel room so I can get changed and then head straight there."

Daniel was taken aback; did she just say *we'll* have to go? Was this woman inviting him to her hotel room?

"I'll call a taxi," she said. "What road are we on?"

"Oh don't worry about it, I'll drive us, my car is only just round the corner."

"Oh OK, well only if you don't mind?"

"Of course not."

They walked back round to his house, he unlocked the car and opened the door for Helena, she lowered herself gracefully in. Before he got in too he quickly checked his watch, it was 17:45. He could not contain his curiosity; he had to check if the case was gone.

With a hint of trepidation he went round to the back of the car and opened the boot.

It was empty.

His eyes opened wide and his pupils suddenly dilated.

This was it.

No turning back.

The deal was on.

He slammed the boot shut and got in the driver's side of the car. He could see that she had some questions about his obsession with the boot but she was choosing not to voice them.

Instead she simply offered, "Everything OK?"

"Yeah fine," he said and tried the key in the ignition.

Nothing happened.

"Shit!" he said, immediately cupping his hand over his mouth and making a very hasty apology for this stray profanity.

"What's wrong?"

"The car won't start, no surprise really, it's been sat here since... well, for nearly seven years. The battery must be dead."

He attempted to turn the engine over a few more times, trying every trick in the book. Holding the clutch down. Trying it in first gear, second. Nothing.

"I'm sorry, we're going to have to get a taxi, I'll call one now."

She smiled as he called a taxi; he told them where to pick up and then when they asked where they were going to he consulted Helena. She told him it was a hotel called the Grand Orchard which he had never heard of. The taxi company told him the routine ten minutes; he thanked them and hung up the phone.

While they were waiting he thought it might be wise to collect some more clothes. He didn't want Helena to see the state of his house but he felt rude asking her to wait outside. Instead he asked her in and ushered her straight into the lounge. It was on the opposite side of the house to his bedroom and as such had survived the inferno relatively unscathed. You didn't need to see the damage to know it was there however, the repugnant stench still hung in the air and Daniel found it hard to hide his embarrassment.

He told her he would only be a moment and headed for the utility room.

"Do you have anywhere to stay?" He could hear her muffled shout ringing through the house.

"I'm fine!" he shouted back.

"I didn't ask if you were fine, I asked if you had anywhere to stay."

He re-emerged at the door to the lounge. "No, but don't worry about it, I'll sort something out."

"You can just stay with me."

His face was washed with disbelief.

"Don't worry!" she said in a reassuring tone. "My room at the hotel has a separate bedroom from the main room; I'm not propositioning you or anything."

He was not the type of person to accept help from anybody, but he could not deny that this gave him the perfect excuse to spend more time with her. "OK then," he relented, "thanks."

He looked back at her and caught a triumphant smile on her face.

The taxi arrived and they left the house together. After a few turns Daniel realized he had no idea where they were going. By his best guess they were still only five minutes or so away from the town centre but he had not seen any of these roads before. Just ahead lay a roundabout which was signposted straight ahead for the motorway. The taxi took a right and they found themselves on a country road, with nothing but a few vague lights in the distance. As they approached the lights Daniel was able to discern the shape of a building and when they were even closer he could see the sign "Grand Orchard".

The building was massive. Daniel could not comprehend how he did not know it was there or in fact where *there* was. He decided he would not give Helena the chance to pay this time, so in a mirror of her stunt from the café Daniel did not wait for the taxi to even come to a complete stop before practically throwing a £10 note at the driver.

They got out of the taxi and Daniel stood glaring at the hotel with the wide-eyed amazement of a child at the gates of Disney World.

"Shall we go in?" Helena chimed in.

The inside of the hotel was even more lavish than the exterior. A huge chandelier hung high above the expansive reception area. The main desk was staffed with two women and a man all impeccably turned out and each busying themselves with a client or a task on the computer system. It couldn't have been more different than his choice of accommodation for the previous night.

"Welcome back, Miss Alkaev." One of the women from the reception raised her head and gave a welcoming smile. "How are you this evening?"

"I'm very well thanks and you, Sophie?" Daniel was impressed that Helena had the courtesy to know the staff by name, a subtle art that so many now ignore.

"Very good thank you, enjoy your evening."

"You too."

They headed for the lifts; the hotel had only six floors which surprised Daniel as from the outside it looked much larger. Helena pressed the button for the sixth floor. Just as the door was about to close a small framed man in a very nice suit jumped into the lift. His face lit up upon seeing Helena.

"Ahhhh, Helena." He spoke with a French accent. "Bon soir, ca va?"

"Michel! Ca va merci, ca va?"

"Ca va."

"Trois?"

"Oui, trois merci."

Daniel had done a little French in high school so he could still grasp the pleasantries and that he wanted to go to the third floor. Had they however conversed any further he would have been well and truly lost. Thankfully for him this was not the case. They rode the lift in silence until the third floor where Michel exited with a brisk, "A bientot."

They continued in the lift up to the sixth floor. When they got out of the lift they were on a small corridor which had only five doors, one of which was for the stairwell. Daniel figured that the whole floor must be dedicated to only four suites. Helena led the way to room 603, opened the door and gestured for Daniel to enter.

She put the key card in the reader by the door and the room was suddenly illuminated. It was palatial. A large open fireplace dominated the right hand wall and there were three large sofas in a C shape around a coffee table where there were a few books scattered.

Helena asked him to make himself at home while she went to get changed. He sat down on the couch directly opposite the fire and looked at the books on the table. He didn't know much about languages but even with his limited knowledge he could see that there were at least two languages other than English represented here.

One of them was written with characters that he didn't even recognize; he imagined that one was Russian. Another read *Män som hatar kvinnor* with the author Stieg Larsson. Daniel was sure he recognised that name from somewhere but he could not recall where. As he sat and waited his curiosity gradually got the better of him.

"So, just how many languages do you speak?" he shouted through to the other room.

"What do you mean?" she said appearing at the door. She had changed and was now wearing a pair of jeans and a black t-shirt; she looked like a completely different person in these more casual clothes.

"Well, obviously English and then French in the lift. I imagine you must speak Czech too? Then there're these books..." he said gesturing to the coffee table. "What is that Russian and... Dutch?"

"Swedish actually," she said matter-of-factly. "You may know it, it's called *The Girl With The Dragon Tattoo* in England."

That was where Daniel knew it from! "Oh yeah, so why do you have it in Swedish?"

"Well I have recently learned Swedish and wherever possible I like to read things in the language they were written in. No matter how good the translation something will always be lost from the author's intentions. Take even the title; it translates literally into *Men Who Hate Women*. A much darker feel all together, wouldn't you say?"

Daniel nodded. "So you never answered my original question. How many languages do you speak?"

"Well that depends on what you refer to as speak. I mean I could exchange pleasantries with Michel in the elevator out there, but had he have wanted to talk about politics or economics I would have been at a loss."

"So how many languages can you talk politics or economics in then?"

She thought for a moment before giving her answer. "Five," she said nonchalantly.

"Five!?!" Daniel exclaimed. "What are they?"

"Russian, Czech, Latvian, English and Swedish."

"Oh my God, that's amazing, how did you learn all those?"

"Please," she said modestly, it's not that amazing. My parents would often talk to me in their native tongues, and all through school I was taught Czech and English, so that covers four of them."

"And what about Swedish?"

"I just fancied learning something different a few years back. As it turns out Swedish isn't as different from English as you might expect. I'm thinking of learning something like Arabic or Mandarin next."

Daniel was seriously impressed, apart from the miniscule amount of French he remembered from school and the odd bit of Klingon he had gleaned from being a serious Trekkie his language skills included English and, well, English.

"Anyway," she continued, "you'll have to excuse me, I just need to go do my hair. If you want a drink please help yourself, I think there's some beer in the fridge."

Daniel wasn't much of a drinker but he thanked her out of politeness. He couldn't help but think that her hair looked perfect just the way it was.

She returned to her bedroom but she wasn't gone for very long at all. "Are you about ready to go?" she asked whilst walking between the two rooms.

Before he opened his mouth Daniel turned to see Helena standing in the doorway and thought he was looking at someone completely different. She was wearing the exact same outfit as a moment ago only instead of her long blonde hair she had short, black hair. Cut to a variety of different lengths and with a one sided fringe that had an electric blue streak running through it.

"Is something wrong?" she asked, clearly concerned by the look on Daniel's face.

"No, it's just... how did you... your hair..."

"Oh that!" she said as if she had just changed her t-shirt. "I have alopecia." Again spoken like it was nothing. "I wear wigs, this is the one I want for tonight's gig."

"Wow," he said amazed. She looked at him for elaboration. "You're just so... so casual about it, I'm surprised."

"Well I have been like this for quite some time now, it wasn't anywhere near as easy at first. I thought about all the ways it could affect me in the future and about how I would never have the same great experiences I had in the years before."

"And how did you come to terms with it then?"

"Well, my mother always had this saying, in English it goes something like 'You should always try to learn from your past, and always try to look forward to your future, but *never* at the expense of experiencing your present.'"

"Your mother sounds like a very wise woman."

"Yes, I think of both of my parents as a blessing, they were both extremely strong people, in very different ways."

They stood in silence for a moment; Daniel just could not get over how full of life this woman was, even in the face of such a life altering condition. Everything she talked about she did with vehemence, but it was more than just what she said and how she said it, there was a fire burning deep inside her eyes; a passion of untold depths that Daniel wanted nothing more than to just grab hold of. She was alive and what was more than that was somehow, even in such a small space of time she had made him feel alive too.

He could not describe it, it was almost as if all the damage he had caused for himself over the years, all the walls, the defences he had built up, they were crumbling down. But it was not through canons, mortars or brute force that they were being torn down, but through words, emotions and a glimpse of a dream.

Once again she interrupted his thoughts. "We'd best get going."

Reluctantly he agreed. This was the second such moment that had occurred and he didn't know if they would get another one. He wanted to desperately cling on to it. To make time stop and just stay there engrossed in this utterly confounding siren. They left, Daniel all the while hoping that this was the beginning and not the end.

13

They got a taxi which took them back into town; Daniel was quietly comfortable being back in familiar surroundings. The small number of bars and clubs which the town had were all confined to a small area off the bottom end of the high street. During his brief relationship with Tara he had frequented a couple of these places so they could spend time "not talking".

The square had recently been pedestrianized so the taxi driver dropped them off at the end of a small path that led through to the main area. Daniel paid the driver without giving Helena a chance again and they walked over to the square.

Helena led the way to a bar called Papillon, one that Daniel was not familiar with. She had a brief talk to the doorman and they were allowed in, seemingly without charge.

The inside was all low lighting and al fresco wall art. The palette of colours on the wall was in places as loud as the music blaring through the sound system. It was a very unusual venue indeed. There was a large bar taking up the majority of the wall which the entrance was on. The centre of the room was a long open dance floor leading to a stage at the end, currently home to a DJ, but there was a curtain behind him through which you could see the silhouette of a full band's worth of instruments. What made the room more unusual was the booth style seating that lined both of the side walls. The venue looked like it couldn't decide whether it was a club or a gig venue, yet somehow it all came together.

"Can I get you a drink?" Helena bellowed over the music.

"No, it's OK, I'll get them. What would you like?"

"I'd love a Corona."

"No worries." He headed straight for the bar, expecting Helena to come too. She instead headed over to a group of people who were loitering at the side of the dance floor. Normally Daniel would feel uncomfortable with this sort of thing, bars were not exactly his scene and being left standing alone in one was even less ideal. Thankfully before he had a chance to feel out of place he glanced over to her and she shot him a disarming smile that put him instantly at ease.

He ordered a Corona for Helena and got an orange juice for himself. He paid the bartender and left a generous tip. Helena saw that he had finished at the bar and broke away from the group to rejoin him.

Any attempts at conversation were near impossible with the loud volume of the music so instead they both sipped their drinks and watched the DJ on the stage. Every now and then they would look at each other and smile Daniel found himself the whole time longing to be somewhere where he could talk to her more. He was enjoying the music but would much rather be listening to her.

The DJ wrapped up his set and the lights were turned down low. Something was played through the system that sounded like an amplified heart beat which gradually got faster and faster. Everyone in the crowd clapped along in time to the heartbeat so as it got faster they were whipped up into a frenzy of applause and cheering.

A bright white light began to flash and with each successive pulse the silhouetted instruments on stage were manned one by one. When everyone was in place the light flashed quicker to an almost strobing effect; the curtain was pulled up and the drummer kicked things off with a crash. The music was fast and energetic, then when the vocalist kicked in it all slowed down and it was more like hip hop than rock. The crowd were moving in time and Daniel couldn't help but get caught up in it. The rhythm was infectious and he had no choice but to move. He glanced to Helena to see her getting truly involved. He found himself so entranced by her movements that he forgot all about everyone else around. He couldn't care how he looked and he didn't need alcohol to shed his inhibitions, he was drunk on her.

They danced side by side for the whole song with each beat Daniel fighting his urges to move closer to her, to dance *with* her. He wanted to take her in his arms, to match the rhythm of her body with his, but the song was over way too soon. The crowd gave out a huge applause and the band introduced themselves as Slippery Ace which was met with even more cheering. Daniel had never been to a gig before but he found himself getting completely caught up in the atmosphere.

Helena turned to look at him; she was still clapping frantically with an enormous grin on her face. She gave him a look that suggested the question "what do you think?" He smiled enthusiastically back and nodded his head. Truth be told he was having a better time than he could have imagined. He had been reluctant about the whole thing at first and had only agreed to come as a way to spend more time with Helena, but here he was now having a new experience and lapping up every minute of it.

The band crashed into another song, this time with a highly reggae infused backbone to it. The crowd bounced rather than danced and Daniel found himself caught up in yet another hypnotic movement. Occasionally Helena would bump into him, he would attempt to apologise immediately but the look in her eyes said that her actions had been deliberate. She was playing with him and she wanted him to play back.

Daniel was a bag of nerves. Historically he had never had any trouble talking and interacting with women *unless* he was interested in them and this was definitely the case here. He wanted to flirt back but his movements felt suddenly laboured and awkward, as if he had forgotten even how to stand and was doing it for the first time. He caught a breath, attempted to relax and tried once more to merge into the rhythm of the pulsating crowd.

The rest of the set went by with no more than a few coy flirtations passed between the two of them. Daniel wished desperately that he could muster the courage to take things further but that didn't seem to be on the agenda for this evening. He continued to focus on the music and to not forget to smile on cue whenever she looked at him.

When the set was over and the final bout of uproarious applause had died down Helena took him by the hand and led him through the crowd outside. Finally they were somewhere where they could talk again.

Before Daniel had a chance to open his mouth Helena made the first move. "So what did you think?" She was still shouting as their ears began to adjust to the quieter volume of the world outside the bar.

"I'm gonna be honest," he said shouting too, "it's not like anything I've ever heard before. But surprisingly I absolutely loved it!"

"Oh that's great!" she said, her smile beaming wide. "I wasn't sure how you would like it. I've loved these guys for a couple of years now."

They stood in silence for a moment, she was stood with her arms wrapped tightly around herself, outside the club was much quieter but also significantly colder. Daniel without asking removed his jacket and placed it affectionately around her shoulders. She smiled and said thanks. "So, do you want to go for another drink somewhere? Or would you prefer to just grab a taxi back to the hotel?"

The hotel? Daniel had forgotten all about the hotel. "I'm easy," he said trying to play it cool. "What would you prefer?"

"I think we should just head back, it's been a busy day. Plus you need your sleep if you're going to show me the sights tomorrow!"

She was so cheeky, yet interminably alluring at the same time. He was excited about the prospect of spending another day with her. More time would surely increase his chances of getting another moment where they might kiss.

Suddenly he remembered about the hospital appointment. "Shit!"

"What's wrong?"

"Oh, nothing, I just have this check up at the hospital which I totally forgot about, it's tomorrow morning at 9:00." He couldn't believe he had even mentioned it, if he had just kept his mouth shut he could have skipped out on the appointment so long as only he knew about it. Surely he had lost his chance now.

"Right, well we'd definitely better get back to the hotel then. Especially if we're going to get breakfast together before we get you to your appointment..."

"But…" he began.

"But nothing, I've decided and you're not going to leave a helpless tourist all stranded and alone now are you?"

This was a medley of sarcasm and charm with a sprinkling of genuine desire. For the first time he allowed himself to believe that her feelings were reciprocal and more than just simple flirting.

He gave her a smile that let her know she'd won and they headed out to find a taxi.

14

The taxi ride back to the hotel was over in no time at all. They got back and made their way up to the room. On the way back they had continued to talk about the gig. Helena was speaking spiritedly about all the other bands she would like to see and how she too was an aspiring musician, doing acoustic stuff mostly just in small cafés. They were still talking about this when they got back to the room. They both took a seat at opposite ends of the couch facing the fireplace.

"So you can speak all these languages AND play guitar and sing? Where on earth do you find all the time to do these things?"

"Daniel please, it's not as if I'm some musical genius or anything, I just play a little bit of guitar and write the odd song." Her modesty seemed sincere. "Anyway, I travel a lot, I spend a lot of time on planes, which gives me plenty of time to read and learn new things."

"I'm just so impressed, I wish I was the creative type, all I can do is science and numbers."

"Why would you say you're not creative?"

"Well because I don't play any instruments or sing or paint or any of those things."

"And do you not think that creativity spans further than music or art?"

Daniel merely shrugged at this question.

"My take on creativity," she continued, "is that it is the whole meaning of life."

Daniel's eyes widened at this rather monumental statement. "And how do you figure that?"

"Simple, people confuse life with society's interpretation on it. If travelling has taught me one thing it is that the reason the so called 'quality of life' is so different in each country or even each city is because the people who live there *believe* it to be so.

"In the UK for example people get bogged down with the 9-5 grind. The house, the mortgage, the friends and family commitments and they believe that this is all there is to life. Add to this a few aspirations of the occasional holiday, party or big event and you have the whole picture. So to get away from this many people go travelling as a way to find the adventure, to live the dream. I personally believe that *you are the dream*, not where you are or what you are doing, but who you are and your attitude towards what you are doing."

Daniel was hanging on her every word, he leaned forward on the couch slightly. "But what does all that have to do with creativity?"

"Everything! Creativity is about *how* we do things, anything. If you feel stuck in your job then is there a creative way which you can mix things up? Doctors treat their patients every day following procedures but the ones who are heralded as ground breaking are the ones who take the procedures and approach them in a new and creative way. You talk of maths and science, those fields are both full of creativity.

"The same is true the other way too. Do you think everyone who has ever written a song or designed a building was a creative person? These people are just as prone to being unimaginative as the person that goes through entering data on autopilot. In fact in my eyes they are worse, because they masquerade round as being creative which just further skews society's take on creativity!"

"Wow! You seem to be quite passionate about this."

"Look I'm no role model. I just could never be like that, grinding away day in day out. I need to be learning something, to a certain extent it doesn't matter what, it could be music or it could be learning better to understand myself and my emotions. I don't think I'm any better than people who do go through the grind, it's just not for me."

"Well I wish I could be more like you. I have to admit I've been locked into some pretty damaging routines for a long time now."

"Like what?"

"Well up until yesterday I was definitely a slave to my job. Not that I ever felt oppressed or anything, I mean I just turned up every day and played my part. But after I returned to work I never did anything different on a daily basis. Even this one day has already shown me a world outside my window that I didn't even know was there, I guess I have you to thank for that."

He smiled but he was thinking about Izzy again, or more specifically the feeling of losing her that had hit him every morning until this day. Strangely he felt he wanted to confide in Helena about this. No one knew about the mornings, not a soul. The more Daniel thought about it the more he realised that this was the one thing that had been holding him back more than anything. If there was one master that he was a slave to it was this morning ritual. So for the first time in seven years he decided to open his heart.

"But I guess," he started tentatively, "the biggest constraint on me has been my mornings…"

She looked at him perplexed.

"Every morning I go through this goddamned routine. It's like the day of Izzy's accident gets played on repeat and I have no control over it. In fact I don't even know it's happening at the time, not until I snap out of it. It's the same thing every day.

"I remember that day as if it was yesterday. Even though we had been getting woken by Rachel every morning since she was born I had never bothered to turn off my alarm. I remember being surprised when it went off, but for some reason I didn't check on either of them, I guess I just wanted Izzy to get some rest so I shut off the alarm after the first snooze and then quietly as I could I got up and made breakfast."

Their eyes were locked intensely as he retold this story and would only be broken when Daniel occasionally glanced away as if to access a distant memory.

"I wanted to surprise her with breakfast in bed, but she woke up before I finished making it. She left the baby asleep and for the first time since the birth we had breakfast as just the two of us. Rachel woke shortly afterwards and I started to get ready for work while Izzy fed her. I kissed them goodbye, and that was the last time I ever saw them."

He was fighting hard to hold back his emotions. Helena had not been so successful. Tears were streaming down her face and her lips and jaw were shivering as if she were ice cold.

She tried her best to muster some words. "That's awful. How did you ever cope with that?"

"I didn't," he said. "As I said I relive this every morning and when it gets to the part where Izzy should walk in... well I just crash. It's like the pain of the first day is still there, undiminished and ready to be called upon at a moment's notice. Ironically this morning is the first time it hasn't happened."

"Why is that ironic?"

"Oh nothing." He tried to backpedal. He may be ready to talk about the morning, but he just couldn't think of how to tell her or anyone about the arrangement on his life that had been made. How could anyone even bear that much information, let alone understand it?

She was still crying so he moved to her side of the couch and put his arm round her again, this time pulling her head into his chest. He found himself gently stroking the side of her face and whispering that everything was all right. It was barely five minutes before she had fallen asleep right there in his arms.

15

He awoke in the morning when the sun came streaming through the window. Helena was still sleeping on him only now on his lap. He figured they must have been like that all night. He had slept sat up with his head craned back and his neck was now extremely stiff.

He glanced down at Helena who was still sleeping peacefully. He wanted to just stare at her for an eternity but it seemed that his gaze on her signalled that it was time too for her to wake.

"Good morning, stranger," she said with a smile and squinted eyes. "Have we been here all night?"

"Yes, you fell asleep and I didn't want to disturb you, I think I must have dropped off myself shortly afterwards."

"What time is it?" she asked rubbing her eyes.

Daniel glanced at his watch and strained his eyes through the morning sun. "It's just before eight."

"Wow! We'd better start getting ready if we're going to make it to your appointment," and quick as a flash she was on her feet and heading for the bedroom as if her energy supply was operated by the flick of a switch.

"If it's too much hassle I can just go by myself and catch up with you later?" Daniel called after her.

"Oh no don't worry about it. I'll just grab a quick shower, it's not like I need to wash my hair." And with that last remark she gave a playful wink; Daniel still wasn't sure how to take jokes about her condition.

Five minutes later she was back at the door to her room wrapped in a towel and without her wig. "Do you need to use the shower?"

She was grinning excitedly and somehow without any hair she was even more alluring. Daniel literally found himself breathless, not through surprise but through attraction. It was like her face was the world's most beautiful picture, so perfect in fact that to frame it would be adding something unnecessary.

"Well?" she said, waiting for an answer.

Daniel regained control of his wide eyes. "Yes, that would be great."

She stayed stood in the doorway as he grabbed his backpack and headed for the bathroom. As he went to pass her she turned her body towards him provocatively, arching her back slightly into the doorway. He wanted desperately to reach out and grab her, to pull her tight into his body and encase her in his arms. He had a vision of her towel dropping to the floor and him running his hands over her bare back. Never before in his life had he been so controlled, consumed even, by his thoughts.

Back in reality he smiled shyly and made his way past her without any physical contact. She gave a little sulk but she couldn't keep her face straight and it soon returned to her beautiful smile. Daniel continued on his way to the bathroom without saying a word.

He locked the door and opened the shower. He spent a moment or two just hunched over the sink trying to regain control of his feelings. When he jumped in the shower it was already steaming hot from when Helena had used it, he lowered the temperature as he figured a cold shower would probably be a prudent choice right now.

He grabbed some of the generic hotel shower gel and began to wash himself. His mind still rife with fantasies about this mysterious woman who had come crashing so uncontrollably into his life. As he washed he fantasised about her hands being the ones washing him, about the two of them in the shower together, nothing but a blur of soap and steam. He tried as hard as he could to shake these thoughts, but the more he fought against them, the stronger they got.

He turned the temperature of the water right down in order to rinse; the icy cold water hitting him like a thousand knives, penetrating his skin and his senses. He tried to cradle himself for warmth but it was useless, the cold of the water was so complete that he had no choice but to surrender to it. Despite the torturous shock of the icy blasts it did have the desired effect, it was all he could think about to get out and get wrapped up in a towel. He had his thoughts back; they belonged to him once more, for now anyway.

He dried himself and picked out some underwear and a t-shirt from his rucksack. He got dressed wearing the same jeans as the day before; he wished he had figured to bring more trousers and not just t-shirts and underwear. He wiped away some of the condensation that had formed on the mirror and stared at his face.

As he stood there he started to feel a familiar tickle in his throat, a split second later he was taken over by another coughing fit. It was much less severe than the one the day before and for this Daniel was extremely grateful. He still felt like a mess though.

Thankfully he had remembered his toothbrush and his hair gel. He spent a few minutes or so grooming himself and then he unlocked the door and stepped out into the bedroom. What he saw next he just could not believe.

Helena was stood in front of the mirror wearing another long flowing dress, similar to the one of the day before. He was looking at the floor when he walked through the door but when he saw her he began to move his eyes up her frame, slowly taking in every inch of her. Her long slender legs, the beautiful natural curves of her body accentuated by her dress and at the very top there it was:

The long flowing red hair.

The same hair from his dream.

It *was* her.

"You look like you've seen a ghost," she said. "I hope you're not going to be this surprised every time I change my hair. I do it quite often!"

"No I'm sorry it's just that you look…" Surely he was not going to tell her she looked like the woman of his dreams. "You look so beautiful."

She blushed and turned her head away bashfully. "Don't be silly."

"I'm being serious, you're stunning!" First beautiful and now stunning? The complements were just rolling out of him. He knew he needed to control his tongue before it got him in any trouble.

"Well... thank you," she said with a hint of disbelief still in her tone. "So are we going to get to your appointment then?"

Daniel looked at his watch, they were going to be late, there was no question about it but he figured it would be best to just get the whole thing over and done with. "Yeah, I suppose we'd best get a move on."

They headed down to the lobby and out to get a taxi. Daniel couldn't remember the last time he had gotten so many taxis. He lived walking distance from work and if he ever wanted to go further afield there were always buses and trains.

As they drove he realised that again he had not been controlled by the ritual today. That was two days running. The day before had not been a fluke. He did have these new morning coughing fits, but even they seemed to be going.

They got to the hospital ten minutes late for his appointment. He hurried to the counter to check in, apologising profusely. The lady at the counter informed him there was no harm done as there would be a slight wait time anyway. This turned out to be only a few minutes, Daniel was called in to see the doctor and Helena waited outside.

"OK, Mr Brady, so how are you feeling?"

Daniel had to cast his thoughts to his health now as the temptation to say "great" or "confused" or "smitten" was too strong. "I feel fine," he arrived on.

"Have you been coughing a lot?"

"Not really, only a little bit in the morning yesterday and then again when I returned to my house. It's getting less each time."

"OK, that's good," the Doctor said making some notes. "And was there any phlegm?"

"The first time yes." Daniel felt quite uncomfortable describing it. "It was green and black, but it was just the once."

"OK, this all sounds very promising, but just to be on the safe side I would like you to go for a chest X-ray. If you take this card down the hall and then to the left you can get booked in. Then when it is complete return here and knock on door 4."

He did as he was instructed. Helena practically shadowed him the whole time moving between waiting areas. Surprisingly this was his first ever X-ray. He had been just as active as many of his friends growing up and he remembered that most of them had X-rays for something or other. Pete McMillan had broken his arm falling off a fence and Toby Roth had broken a couple of fingers with a terrible display of goal keeping one time. They had a great day in school when he had brought in the pictures; even then Daniel always found science stuff to be highly interesting.

He sat on the stool and waited while the technician positioned all manner of shields and contraptions around him. He was fascinated by the whole ordeal and had it been under better circumstances would have loved to have asked a few questions.

The X-ray was over extremely quickly, Daniel asked how long he would have to wait before the prints were available and the technician informed him they were digital now and would be arriving on the doctor's screen almost immediately. Daniel was sufficiently impressed by this.

He made his way back and knocked on door number 4, a nurse opened up and let him in, he sat and waited for the doctor.

"OK, Mr Brady," the doctor said, appearing magically from behind the curtained end of the room. "I have had a look at your X-rays and I am happy to discharge you today, would that be alright with you?"

"Yes, absolutely," Daniel replied enthusiastically.

"OK then. Are you a gym goer, Mr Brady?"

"No, not really." He hadn't been to the gym or in fact done any sort of formal exercise in as long as he could remember. That being said he was in pretty decent shape, a fact which he accredited to not using the car.

"Alright, well either way I would not advise you to undertake any strenuous cardiovascular activity for at least a couple of weeks. Also keep an eye on that cough, if it persists I would advise you to see your GP. Or if it is quite severe present yourself at A&E. Is that clear?"

"Yes, doctor."

"OK, well that's all, unless you have any further questions?"

"No, I'm all good, thank you, doctor."

"My pleasure."

Daniel headed back out into the waiting area and gave two thumbs up to Helena who smiled back excitedly; it was clear from the look on her face that she was genuinely concerned for his health and not just playing her part. For this Daniel was truly grateful.

16

With the hospital visit all done and dusted Daniel was left with a new challenge – being Helena's tour guide. He had to admit he was stumped; there really wasn't much to see in this town and he figured that even if you walked it you could see the majority of the area in just a few short hours.

"So what would you like to see?" he said trying to place the ball back into her court.

"I don't know, you're the local, what would you recommend?" OK so the responsibility was back with him again.

"Well it really depends on what you're into. There's really not all that much to see but if you're into history then we do have a small museum. Or if architecture is more your thing then perhaps the town hall and the law courts would be more enjoyable? They're the closest things to classic buildings we have around here. Failing that as I mentioned yesterday there are plenty of parks."

"Yes."

"Yes to which one?"

"To all of them," she said, her smile growing ever wider. She had her hands cupped together and was swaying gently from side to side. Her mannerisms had an innocent almost childlike quality to them at times that just made Daniel want to protect her, he wasn't sure what from exactly but he already felt as if he would lay down his life before letting her come to any harm.

"OK then," he agreed finally. "I hope you're wearing comfy shoes though, 'cause the best way to see all this stuff is on foot."

They walked around the town for hours and soon it was more like Daniel that was being taken on a tour. Every road they would pass she would ask, "What's down here?" and

Daniel would always have to answer embarrassedly that he did not know.

"My father once told me that you should always glance down every side street. As you never know what you will find. I think that's how I got into travel writing. I would keep a diary as a child and I would often go on little 'adventures' all by myself. I would walk around my hometown and just head off down random roads that I had never been down before. Then I would write all about them in my diary later that night."

"What sort of things would you write?"

"Oh allsorts, if someone had an unusual garden ornament, a scary plant or a friendly cat, that sort of thing. Once I found this really old abandoned house with a massively overgrown garden. The place was practically falling apart but I'll never forget that as I looked into the garden I saw a single red rose, the deepest crimson you can imagine, sat right there living amongst all the weeds. It was so beautiful; I wish I had a camera back then."

Daniel thought back to what she had said the previous day about there always being something going on if you look for it. How many times had he been down these roads and not even glanced down these streets, let alone walk down any of them? It made him wonder what else he had been missing out on all this time.

Helena had a compact camera with her and was taking photos of anything and everything. Occasionally she asked Daniel to stand or pose for her. Every time he would try and talk his way out of it and every time she would get her photo, it seemed his feeble protests were falling on deaf ears.

Without even realising it Daniel had led them to the house that he grew up in. He hadn't been down this road since his parents decided that their suburb wasn't quite far enough from the city and upped sticks to the West Country. It was a medium sized house, a three bedroom semi-detached with a small front garden and a slightly larger garden at the rear. It looked almost exactly as it had done when his parents had owned it except there was a small consort of garden gnomes sat beneath the overhang of the bay window. If there was one thing Daniel had never understood it was garden gnomes.

"Oh my gosh!" he said, significantly louder than he had intended to.

"What is it?"

"This used to be my parents' house, I grew up here."

"Wow, so this is where the great Daniel Brady became the man that he is today?" There was nothing caustic about the way she said this and Daniel could not comprehend how she could make such a statement and still sound sincere.

"I wouldn't go that far, but yeah, I learned to walk and to talk right in this very house."

"We need to get a picture of you here."

"No way!"

"Oh come on, how often do you come back to the place you grew up? We *have* to do this."

"But what if the owners are in? Will they not find it strange that a couple of random people are taking pictures on their front lawn?"

"Who cares, it will be done in a sec. Oh and who said we were a couple?" Her face grew suddenly very serious

"That's not what I meant. I errrr, just meant a couple as in two... two people... not a couple."

She flashed him a quick grin that succinctly said she had been pulling his leg. "So are you going to pose for the picture or do I need to go and knock on the door and ask for permission?"

"No don't do that! I'll have the picture, just make it quick, OK?" She had won again.

She took the picture and then immediately took another one when Daniel dropped his pose, she had done that a few times during the course of the day and Daniel thought he had figured out why – she wanted to try and capture him while he wasn't posing too, to get a more natural shot, he had done the same trick back in the day with Izzy.

"You do realise you're going to have to come to Prague with me now, don't you?"

"How do you figure that?"

"Well now that I've seen the house you grew up in, don't you think it's only fair that I show you mine?"

Daniel was at a loss for words, he didn't 100% know if this was a serious statement or not and he did not want to appear a fool if he showed his excitement only to be the victim of a practical joke. Instead he merely suggested that they continue with their tour.

Around 13:45 Helena led them down another side street where they found a small café. It was becoming quite worrying just how much of his town Daniel didn't know about. They stopped to rest their feet briefly and get some lunch. Helena ordered coffee and a club sandwich with some dill pickle; Daniel ordered a fresh orange juice and a baked potato with tuna and sweet corn.

The conversation wasn't huge over lunch. Helena spent some time flicking through the photographs on her camera and showing Daniel some of her favourite ones. A lot of the ones she showed involved animals and a few were of people who didn't know they were having their photo taken.

"I just love shots like these," she said.

"Do you not feel weird taking someone's picture without their permission?"

"No not really, I mean it's often impossible not to, imagine you're in a crowd for example or you're taking a picture of a friend at a tourist attraction. There's always going to be other people in those pictures unless you take an extreme close up or get really lucky!"

"That's not the point though is it?"

"Isn't it? The other people are still on the picture, so if it's a privacy thing then they're just as much infringed upon by being in the background as by being the subject."

"Well I suppose if you put it that way."

"I do!" she said abruptly but with a cheeky glint in her eye. They sat and looked through the photos while they waited for their food. When it came they both ate at an extremely leisurely pace. Daniel couldn't remember the last occasion he had taken such time over his lunch. A little flag in his mind kept reminding him that his time on earth was short but mostly he just pushed it aside. For now he was just going to sit and take his time, over lunch, over life, over her.

17

When they had finished lunch they continued on with the tour. Daniel showed her the town hall and courthouse and she took yet more photos. They found themselves back on the high street and true to form Helena wanted to take a quick peek down every side street. They turned onto one called Riley Crescent, which appeared to be a cul-de-sac leading to just about nowhere. This did not seem to deter Helena's curiosity though and she headed down full steam ahead.

About halfway down the road they happened upon a small used bookshop.

"Ooooooh do you mind if we go in?" Helena said spiritedly.

"Yeah sure, but you know there's a Waterstones on the high street, you're more likely to find whatever you're looking for there."

"That really depends on what you're looking for doesn't it? Anyway I love old bookstores, there's something magical and romantic about them, don't you think?"

Daniel didn't think. He thought there was something cramped and smelly about them, but he decided to play along anyway. "Sure, why not."

The bookshop was fairly small inside but the shelves ran floor to ceiling and were packed tight with thousands of different books. There was a man who appeared to be in his 60s sat on a stool behind the counter with a thick pair of reading glasses balanced precariously on the end of his nose. He was drinking tea from an old china cup and appeared to be reading a large leather bound book of some description.

Helena pored over every shelf, taking in each and every tome contained within. Daniel thought he would use the opportunity to see if there was anything here that might interest him, some of Steven King's earlier work perhaps, but really he was just browsing aimlessly to give her the time to do what she wanted. He knew buying anything would be pointless; he would never get the chance to read it.

Unlike many other similar thoughts that day this particular thought had a strange knock-on effect in his head; feelings were surfacing that had not been there since he resolutely placed the case of money in the boot of the car. There was apprehension, doubt, maybe even regret there. He thought of all the things he would never do, paradoxically he had booked a holiday the day before that he would never ever take. He would never get to see where things could lead with this enchanting woman, never finish another book or see another city, never see his parents again, his parents! He hadn't seen them in years and had managed just the briefest of conversations over the phone around birthdays and Christmas and here he was lamenting the loss of a relationship he had long been neglecting.

His mind was quickly giving way and it wasn't long after that his body started to follow. First his breathing quickened, it was like all the oxygen had been sucked out of the room, he felt like he was back in the fire, surrounded by air but none of it breathable. His legs went next and he collapsed forward bracing himself with his hands on a shelf, books spilling out to the sides of his grasp. He had to get outside and quick. Every step was like a miniature fall, like he was slumping his full weight into each one, lurching and swaying, flailing his arms to support his weight on anything that would accommodate him.

Helena turned at the commotion and rushed to his side, but he was already barrelling through the door. He broke through into daylight and fresh air. He flung his head forward and vomited on the pavement, barely even aware of Helena by his side, cradling him at the waist.

She pulled him back to the front of the building and sat him down. She was trying to talk to him, to ask him something but it was as if his ears had been tightly packed with cotton wool. He breathed deeply and tried to count 1... 2... 3... 4. He needed to regain control and fast, all he could think was that he must look like some sort of lunatic.

He was aware of someone else beside him now, it was the owner of the bookshop, he had come to Daniel's aid with some water. Helena took the cup and pressed it to Daniel's lips. He tried to compose himself, to just take one sip, even that seemed to take all the effort in the world. Helena saw him struggling and she tilted the cup to assist.

The cold water hit his lips like a morning alarm, ferrying him back to the world of the waking. The sounds became clearer and he could hear Helena's sweet voice once more.

"Dan, Dan, are you OK, Dan? Try to talk to me."

"I, I, I'm fine," he managed. "I was just feeling a little light headed, that's all." He looked to the store owner and was overcome with embarrassment. "I'm sorry about your books."

"Oh don't worry about it, you gave myself and your girlfriend quite a scare back there."

"Oh she's not my..." he started but before he could correct the man's mistake she jumped in.

"Thank you, Mr..."

"Jacobs," the man answered.

"Mr Jacobs, thank you very much."

"Oh it's nothing, it's just a cup of water. Is there anything else I can do for you? A sugary tea perhaps?"

She turned her attention back to Daniel for a moment. "Sweetie?" Where had that come from? "Would you like to go to the hospital?"

"Oh no no no!" he implored. "I'm perfectly OK, I promise."

"OK, well," she said, this time to the shop keeper, "would it be possible for you to call us a taxi? I think I'd better get him home."

"Yes of course," the man said and was on his feet and into the store quicker than his elderly frame may have suggested was possible.

Helena sat with Daniel and held him in her arms; her touch was tender yet firm and made Daniel feel instantly safe. He could not recall the last time he had been truly held like this. Even in his relationship with Tara they had never been the "hugging type". It felt great, as if this one simple act was removing all the chaos that was so consuming him only a moment earlier.

The store owner returned to say the taxi was on its way and asked again if there was anything more he could do. When they said there wasn't he excused himself and returned to the shop to begin undoing the mess.

Being so close to the high street it didn't take very long at all for the taxi to arrive. Helena first helped Daniel into the back of the car and then once he was secured she returned to the shop to thank the owner once more. She gave the address of the hotel to the taxi driver and they set off.

For the duration of the taxi ride back she pulled his head into her shoulder, hugging him with one arm and stroking his hair affectionately with the other. She didn't say much but she kept angling his face so that she could check he was still OK. He made a few apologies for making an embarrassing scene which she told him was complete nonsense.

They got back to the hotel and she took him by the hand back to the room. She helped him to the couch and instructed him to lie down. He didn't feel this was necessary but did so dutifully anyway.

"Is there anything I can get for you? Tea, coffee, water?" she asked.

"Honestly I'm fine, I don't want you fussing over me, and I'm supposed to be your tour guide remember?" The tone of his voice showed that he wasn't so worse for wear after all, which was a huge comfort to Helena.

"Well if you're sure..."

"I am," he cut in. He was still embarrassed about what had happened and he was determined to, as Johnnie always told him, "man-up".

"OK, well I just need to go to the bathroom, are you sure you don't want anything before I go?"

He shook his head and she got up to go. No sooner had she left and Daniel felt himself drifting off to sleep, the sights and sounds before him slowly fading as his body gave in to the tiring consequences of the day's events.

18

His sleep was far from restful. He was hounded by nightmares. There seemed to be many of them lasting only a few seconds at a time, there was no way of telling if they were all somehow linked in to one. Flashes of reality and fantasy merged together; with scenes taken from the days before mixed confusingly with random images which Daniel could not understand. The hospital, the bookstore, the café, Helena, the mysterious man and his insane offer.

Each of these things flashed up in Daniel's subconscious mind, with no seeming link from one to the next, then as suddenly as they had formed they were all gone. Replaced only by the image of a man, or at least the frame of a man, no face was visible and he/she/it never spoke a word. The only feature that hung in Daniel's mind was the person's purple shoes. Daniel fixated on them and as he did the left foot began to tap on the floor. Quiet and slow at first but with each tap gaining in both volume and velocity. All other sounds were blotted out by this unceasing din and it felt to Daniel as if his head were going to explode.

He woke up with a start and in a cold sweat. It was night time and were it not for Helena being sat at his feet jumping to attention as immediately as he had exited his dream he would have had no idea where he was.

"Is everything OK?" she asked with a seriously concerned tone.

"Huh, wha... yes." He was still a little dazed from the experience. "It was just a nightmare, I'm OK now."

"OK, but you do realise if you keep on giving me these little scares that there will be repercussions, mister!" she said with a cheeky grin.

Daniel felt better for having her by his side and made an effort to sit himself up.

"How long was I out for?" he asked.

"About three hours, I came back from the bathroom to find you out cold and figured it would be best to let you sleep. Especially after the day you've had!"

"I'm sorry, I've been a bit of a burden on you it seems."

"Oh don't be silly, gave me a chance to catch up with some reading anyway. I hope you don't mind, but I ordered us some room service..."

"Oh, gosh, wow." He felt as inexperienced as a teenager again. "Of course I don't mind, I wasn't even expecting to..."

"To what?"

"To be seeing you after our tour, or the poor excuse for one at least."

"Stop being so modest, I had a great time, even with you vomiting over some priceless Mary Shelley novels!"

He smiled, part embarrassed, part ecstatic at further opportunities to spend time with her.

"Anyway," she continued, "I hope you don't think I am being presumptuous, but I just really wanted to have dinner with you, and I didn't want to make plans to go out with you asleep so I just got some room service. I didn't know what you like either so there may be a LOT of food!"

"I like pretty much everything, apart from olives," he said with a nervous laugh.

"Well I'm sure you'll find something you like then."

"I already have," he said and then immediately regretted it. If there was a list of the worst lines in history this would get hall of fame status. He sat in silence hoping that the meaning of what he had just said got lost somewhere in translation.

He searched her eyes, unsure of his next move and at that moment something perfect happened, she stared deeply back into his eyes and cautiously said, "Me too."

They stared at each other intently. They were stood on the threshold of making something more of this chance encounter and despite the apparent green light which had just been given they were both treading carefully.

Their bodies seemed out of synch with their thoughts, a slight lean here, a moment of hesitation there and the whole thing held together by an almost childlike curiosity.

Daniel had no idea where this was heading for Helena, but seriously where could it possibly head for him? He was a marked man, the nightmares of earlier hitting home with that fact: his days were numbered. What was he thinking engaging with another human being? Was it not his social responsibility to just keep a low profile for a few days, minimise the effects of the aftermath that would surely follow his demise. The thoughts were there again, just as they were in the bookstore and they were holding him prisoner.

But then one final thought came into his head, both powerful and transient. "Fuck it!" There was no time before, no hospital, no strange offers. There was no time after, no future hopes or aspirations. There was only this moment and he was going to take it.

He leaned in fast and then pausing briefly for a second, their lips barely millimetres apart, he took her in his arms and kissed her with every ounce of passion he had left.

And that was all it took to set a chain reaction in place that would change everything. She threw her arms around him and pulled him in even tighter, their bodies melding into one, their lips locked kissing each other furiously, lips lost with lips, tongues clashing and colliding, fighting for space and for impact. Their bodies writhing towards one another rocking with a primal rhythm that transcends conscious thought.

The momentum that had built was cruising along now and their passion was unstoppable like a runaway train hurtling along the tracks at breakneck pace. Fervently they tugged at each other's clothes. Helena moved her hands up and entwined her fingers in Daniel's short hair, his actions were reciprocal and soon he had his fingers knotted within the hair that in this moment he did not care was not her own.

He massaged the back of her head tracing the curvature with his grasp and she in turn lowered her hands so that they were firmly holding his neck. Daniel became aware that one of the shoulder straps of Helena's dress had fallen loose and quickly moved his hand to caress the newly bared flesh. He had never felt so alive, the blood rushing though his veins like traffic on an autobahn.

Their body temperatures were rising and so too was the air around them, the room felt hot and stuffy as if it were beckoning them to shed their clothes. Daniel took a chance and swiftly brushed away the other shoulder strap of Helena's dress. With nothing else to hold it up the dress fell to her waist, exposing her bare breasts, the sight of which caused Daniel's eyes to immediately dilate as his pulse quickened so much that it was a shock even to him.

There were beads of sweat glistening on her chest as she began to unbutton his shirt. He had made a bold move and she had responded in kind. Their passion was palpable, surely nothing could stop them now, they were on a one-way trip to the Promised Land. Or so it seemed when just at the pivotal moment there was a loud knock on the door followed by two muffled yet anticlimactic words:

"Room service."

19

Helena quickly pulled her dress up securing it back around her shoulders and headed for the door. She opened it and the waiter entered pushing a large hostess trolley literally loaded with food.

"Where would you like it?" he asked politely.

"Oh anywhere really," she replied, gesturing to the general area of the couch where Daniel sat looking flustered with a half unbuttoned shirt.

The waiter moved the trolley into place and set about meticulously preparing the ad-hoc dining area. Both Daniel and Helena remained silent while the waiter took his time. Truth be told they both couldn't care less about the presentation of the food but their mutual impatience was kept in check by good old fashioned politeness.

"Enjoy your meals," the waiter said effusively upon finishing. Helena thanked him and saw him to the door, hastily grabbing at some money from the sideboard for a tip.

She closed the door behind him and sunk back against it, looking at Daniel. The embarrassment she had hidden so well while the waiter was in the room now written all over her face.

They both stayed in silence for a moment, neither one really knowing what to say. Finally Helena spoke up. "Well, shall we eat then?" Clearly the moment had passed, Daniel hoped with all his heart it had only been placed temporarily on hold.

He smiled and nodded.

"Can I get you anything to drink?" she asked him. "Wine perhaps?"

"I don't really drink wine…"

Helena looked as if someone had just insulted her. "Well, that's simply not good enough, obviously you've just never had a good bottle!" she said in a way that was equally playful and reprimanding.

"It's just never interested me," he said defensively.

"I'll tell you what," she continued, "I'll pour you a glass, something nice and easy just to get your toes in the pool, and if you don't like it then that will be the last I say of it... What do you say?"

He thought about this for a moment and then replied, "Oh go on then, but you'd best have a glass of water on standby for when I hate it!"

There was a small fridge in the corner of the room disguised as a chest of drawers. It was only marginally larger than a minibar but when she opened it Daniel could see she had a couple of bottles of wine, a few beers and some cans of coke stacked neatly inside. She picked out a bottle of rosé which later Daniel would learn was a white Grenache and placed it on top where there were a couple of wine glasses already.

She opened the bottle and poured two generous glasses, Daniel thought this was a bit excessive for what he believed would only be a "taste".

Before she collected the glasses and returned to him Daniel saw her quickly play with an mp3 player which she then proceeded to plug into a wire on the bureau; the room was instantly filled with music. She smiled, satisfied that everything was good, grabbed the glasses and returned to Daniel on the couch.

She passed one glass to him and held the other aloft. "To new friends!" she toasted.

"To new friends," he echoed. They clinked their glasses and both took a sip. Helena's eyes fixed on Daniel waiting to scrutinize every detail of his reaction.

He wrinkled his brow slightly and took the glass down from his lips. He gave an approving nod that in turn caused Helena to give a smile of relief.

"That's actually not bad," he said, with more than a hint of surprise present in his tone.

"It's a good job I have another bottle then," she said smiling. "Although the other one is a gerwurtstraminer, which you might not be ready for yet, but we'll cross that bridge when we come to it."

"It's a what now?" Daniel said and they both burst out laughing.

The conversation started off a little awkward again at first, but getting back into something really is never as difficult as the baby steps and small talk that are the beginnings of most relationships and pretty soon they were laughing, joking and talking about all manner of things.

There really was a vast choice of food, tempura prawns, potato skins, chicken wings, chicken goujons, various plates of tapas, fries, onion rings. It seemed the restaurant catered to all sorts of styles. They both tucked in enthusiastically as they talked and drank their wine.

Not many of the songs from Helena's mp3 player were familiar to Daniel and more than a handful were sung in foreign languages. On one of them Daniel found himself caught up in the music despite not even knowing what it was being sung about.

"What are they saying?"

"It doesn't really translate literally, but the closest I can say it is, if we can find some comfort in the pain that we suffer, maybe we can discover the key to life. It's a beautiful song about how rather than try to avoid pain we should accept that it is a vital part of life; we should deal with it and learn from it rather than try to pretend it isn't there."

Daniel thought on this for a moment, it felt as though it was talking directly to him. After all had he not ignored his pain for years, turning his back on it daily only for it to catch up on him every single morning? And then finally when the pain became too much to bear and he could avoid it no longer then his idea of dealing with it was to run away in the biggest possible way, the way you can never come back from.

"It's beautiful," he said.

She took his hands in hers and they sat silently listening to the music for a while, gazing into each other's eyes. The next song that came on was in English, but still by an artist Daniel did not know. It appeared to be a song about loss, but not of a lover, the loss of a friend or maybe of self, Daniel couldn't quite figure out which. Each line seemed to bring with it a new message but one particular line that was imprinted onto Daniel's mind went:

No longer focussed on the things I have lost, I won't be thrown out or discarded, left to breakdown and rust.

This line sparked a change deep inside him and he knew all at once that he had to tell Helena everything, about the suicide, about how he feels about her and about what he now wanted more than anything to avoid, his death. He knew he wanted, no needed to tell her, but how could he?

He'd talked to her about some pretty heavy things before, really heavy if you consider the short space of time that they had known each other, but this was different. All those other things had been about things that had happened to him but this… this was something HE had done TO HIMSELF.

He was going to have to say something soon, if not about this then he could try and just say something light hearted. But it was too late, he had been consumed by this overwhelming need to remove the weight of all this from bearing down on him and what's more, it was having a physiological reaction. His heart rate had quickened and just like on the day that started all of this the beads of sweat had already begun to form on his forehead.

The expression on Helena's face changed from one of adoration to that of concern. "Is everything OK?" she asked apprehensively.

He clammed up; he couldn't form a word, not even a single syllable. It was all he could manage to remember to breathe. His thoughts were flitting around from one place to the next; it seemed impossible to catch a single one before the next came swarming into view.

"I've…" he started, this simple word taking a number of seconds to form. "I've got something I need to tell you."

She looked on not saying anything, giving him time to proceed, but no pause was needed. The act of producing that first sentence had opened the floodgates and for the next 40 minutes Helena sat silently as Daniel told her everything. About the seven years after the accident, the morning routine, the endless days of living on autopilot. Those seven years were the easy part, the last few days, well that was something different entirely.

Once he got to Monday in the story everything changed. He was less animated, more pensive and began to justify many things. He realised this was actually just as much for his own benefit as for Helena's. He had hardly had a chance to think over the events of the last few days himself. He told her about losing his job, about losing his temper with his boss and then about the attempted suicide. These were the only parts of the story where she said anything at all and even then she just held her hands over her mouth and said, "Oh my God," which was gasped more than spoken.

He then carried on through the story, to the hospital and the meeting with the stranger and finally to where their stories began to overlap and where he met her and took the briefcase to the car.

After Daniel's lamentation they sat looking at each other. Helena lowered her hands from her mouth where they had been sat for quite some time now and regarded Daniel thoughtfully. He opened his mouth, intent on telling her exactly how he felt about her. How she had come along and made him want to be alive again, to treasure it, the good and the bad, to learn from the pain, to live in the moment, but she never gave him a chance to utter the words. She raised her finger up to stop him from speaking and then slowly pressed it against his lips.

Their eyes were locked furiously for a final moment before she leapt in and threw her arms around him, holding him tighter than he could ever remember being held.

Softly she whispered into his ear, "You don't have to worry about any of that anymore. I'm here, I'm with you now and we'll figure out a way out of this. Together."

She released the hug and got to her feet taking his hand in hers. He got up from the couch and she led him to the bedroom. As they were leaving the room the mp3 player was playing a song by an American band called Jars of Clay with the lyrics "Rescue me from hanging on the line, I won't give up on giving you the chance to blow my mind. Let the 11th hour quickly pass me by, I'll find you when I think I'm out of time."

20

He was awakened the next morning by a tiny sliver of sun sneaking in through the curtains that had just worked its way round to shine in his eye. He squinted and then looked down. The woman to whom he had lost his heart in a matter of days was sleeping peacefully on his chest, a deeply contented smile fixed on her face.

He lay there taking it all in. The bright light creeping in through the window, the last lingering smells of her perfume from the night before, faint but still there. He was happy, but more than that, he was at ease.

The thoughts still swam in his head of the days before but all the sharpness had been removed from them, as if they were the memories of some other Daniel Brady, something he had read once or seen in a film.

He wondered where this sense of calm stemmed from. At first he thought it was due to the three times they had made love the night before. His confession had sparked a flame inside Helena that didn't seem to want to go out. Or perhaps it was hopefulness of what the future may hold. "We'll figure out a way out of this. Together," she had said the night before and he truly believed they would. But then he realised that the reason lay in Helena's mother's saying; he was actually living in the now. He accepted this and decided that this is what he would carry on doing, until she woke up at least.

This came only a few minutes later. She blinked her eyes a few times and then craned her neck back to look at him.

"Morning," she said with a huge smile on her face.

"Morning," he said back, beaming equally wide. "How are you feeling?"

"Fantastic, you?"

"Yeah great, I had an amazing time last night."

"Me too," she said whilst stretching her arms out above her head. "There'll be plenty of time for more later, but first we've got a few plans to make, don't we."

"I guess we do," Daniel said, the tone of his voice was surprisingly cheery considering the grave circumstances behind their yet-to-be-made plans.

They got out of bed, they were both still naked and Daniel hurriedly moved to pull his boxers on.

"What you hiding for? I've seen it all before," Helena said playfully to him before throwing some clothes on herself.

She walked out into the other room and foraged through the remains of last night's banquet for anything that would still be edible this morning. She took a bite of a piece of garlic bread before hastily spitting it back out again. "Hmm, I think we'd best go out for breakfast!"

They both had a quick shower and got ready to leave the room. The physical aspect of their relationship had come on leaps and bounds now and each time they passed each other they would steal a kiss or pinch the other's bum. They were smitten and Daniel was loving it.

They went downstairs and decided to have breakfast in the hotel restaurant. The breakfast was a buffet style but with tea and coffee served at the table. Daniel had a furious appetite after the previous evening's activities. He was initially quite self-conscious about piling his plate high before he saw Helena had already begun creating a large mountain of beans, sausage and bacon on her plate. She flashed him a roguish grin and said, "You gotta get your money's worth."

Daniel couldn't agree more and responded by lumping a further two sausages onto his already overfull plate.

They sat down facing each other with only their twin feasts, two cups of coffee and a glass of orange juice between them. Their eagerness to start making plans was at this moment eclipsed only by their desire to tuck-in. They began to make headway through the mammoth meals before getting down to brass tacks.

When they finally began to speak it was Daniel who spoke first. "So, what do you think I should do?"

"WE should do," she corrected him. "I told you, we're in this together now."

"OK, sorry, what do you think *we* should do?"

"Hmm, I was kind of hoping you would have some ideas."

That momentarily killed the conversation; Daniel had hung his hopes on her having some sort of master plan to get him out of this mess despite him being the one to get in it in the first place. Then suddenly he had an idea. "I've still got the rest of the money, we could easily get away. I mean this Jez guy has got his cash, if I just stay out the way for a while, I'm sure he won't even bother to find me." Then he thought a bit further. "But what about when you go back home? I don't want to do any of this if it's not with you."

"You do know that the Czech Republic is a member of the EU right? You can come with me. Or we could relocate somewhere else... together. We have so many options. Why come back here and take the chance that this guy will one day catch up to you? We could have a new life anywhere we choose."

It was hard not to get swept up in the ideology of it all and Daniel couldn't help but fantasize about a brand new start somewhere else, with the woman of his dreams.

"But," she said, snapping him back to reality, "in the mean time you need to stay away from places you'd regularly go. If everything they knew about you the other night is anything to go on then I think it's safe for us to assume that they will be looking for you. You won't be safe in places they suspect you to be."

"Yeah you're right. What should we do then?"

"Well you should be safe here, I mean after all you only met me after the incident. Other than that I think we just need to get away from here as soon as possible. I should get to the travel agents today and sort something out. Will you be OK to stay here on your own?"

"I'm sure I'll be fine, I mean even if they did know where I was, I highly doubt they'd risk sneaking into a fully staffed hotel and breaking into one of the suites."

"OK, I'll get us a couple of tickets to…" She paused to allow him to volunteer a destination. "Well is there anywhere you would like to go?"

"Don't ask me, you're the travel writer, where would you recommend?"

"I'm not sure, I'll just find something reasonably priced in Europe, it's not the right time of year for beaches so would a city break be OK?"

"Fine by me, don't worry about the price either, you can just take the rest of the cash I have upstairs," he said but not in a boastful way.

"Don't be absurd! I'll pay for this, call it your fee for being such an accommodating tour guide."

"And don't you be absurd, I insist, call it your fee for saving my life, not that anything could ever repay that debt."

They both smiled wistfully and returned their attentions to their breakfast, silently agreeing on the plan afoot.

21

The rest of their morning passed without much consequence. Daniel saw Helena off asserting that she must use his leftover "self inheritance" as he was whimsically calling it and she in turn insisted that he not leave the room until she got back from the travel agent.

He spent the time on his own restlessly, flicking through channels on the TV and leafing through the few of Helena's books that were in a language he could comprehend. He was nervous, the calm of the morning had long left him and he found himself thinking that everything was all running too smoothly.

In his head he kept playing out scenarios in which things would go horribly wrong. Most of these caprices were based so much in the realms of fantasy that no normal person would ever believe them, but then this had been an extremely far-fetched week so far.

He imagined a masked ninja smashing in through the window, killing him where he stood, or a timed explosion bringing the roof of the hotel crashing down on his head. One of the more plausible ideas was that he would merely be left standing there until hotel staff came calling asking him to vacate the room and informing him that Miss Alkaev had checked out and ridden off into the sunset with his money.

He decided to call her.

The phone rang until it was eventually picked up by a voicemail spoken in one of Helena's many other languages.

He hung up and tried again.

And again.

And again.

Nothing.

By now he had started to sweat again and all his insecurities were teaming up on him, coming back together like the reprise in a Broadway musical. Now every shadow was closing in on him and every noise was cause for concern. He paced the room, checking through each of the windows, truly paranoid that he was being watched.

He tried to tell himself that he was just being crazy but it was useless. Why was she not answering her phone? Why had he let her leave with all his money? How was he going to survive now? These thoughts all mingled together to cause one almighty cacophony inside his head when suddenly they were replaced by something else, something more familiar, the sound of his phone ringing. He answered it without a moment's hesitation, still convinced that what awaited him would be bad news.

"Hello?" he said cautiously.

"Hey, you, did you try to get hold of me?"

It was her, she was OK, everything was OK.

"Oh yeah, was just wondering how you were getting on that's all," he said trying to sound nonchalant.

"I'm actually just coming in through the front entrance of the hotel right now," she said, instantly reassuring him. "Sorry I missed your call, I had a very chatty cab driver who wouldn't stop telling me about how if I want to really get to grips with England then I have to watch Top Gear! Anyway I'm just getting in the lift now, I'll see you in a sec yeah?"

"Yeah, cool."

He hung up the phone, took a giant breath in and then released it, his exhalation sweeping the last of the demons from the room. When he regained his composure he couldn't help but smile at just how silly he had been. Moments later he heard the sound of a key card being inserted and the door opened. His love was back and she had brought some Burger King.

"Heyyyy," she said, "by now you must think I'm a pig, I mean I'm always eating right? I just thought you might be hungry."

He gave her a massive smile and he welled up with emotion.

"What's wrong?" she said.

"Nothing, I just missed you so much," he replied, hoping that he didn't sound as clingy as he thought he did. She put the bags down and they shared a giant hug.

"Wanna know a secret?" she said still smiling. "I missed you too."

He kissed her once long and then another four times short before moving his head back to look in her eyes. "So, where are we going then?"

"Well, I wanted to make it quite memorable, so rather than just book one destination I decided to arrange something with what I think is a great starting point for Europe. We start in Paris, then to Barcelona, then a few days in Berlin before spending the weekend in Rome. Then after that as promised I'm going to take you to my home town, Prague."

"Oh my God, that sounds so amazing. I'm gonna need to get some more clothes for all this, we need to go back to my house."

"Absolutely not, mister!" she snapped. "Are you forgetting the most important thing about our plan? No going to places you're expected to be! We're going to some of the shopping capitals of Europe too, you can get clothes as we go!"

"I guess so, I thought you were gone for a while, no wonder when you've booked such a complex trip. So when do we head off? Do I need to lay low for a while?"

"That's the best bit! I managed to get us some tickets for tomorrow!" At this point she jumped up and down clapping like a teenage girl and Daniel couldn't blame her. This was all so fantastic; they were going to have the adventure of a lifetime. It was such a paradox thinking that only two days earlier he was booking a holiday he would never take, listening to the excitement and even jealousy in the travel agent's voice yet feeling no excitement himself. And here he was now, with a completely different journey, but one much more tangible sat right ahead of him.

"So," she continued, "just one night of lying low, a taxi to the airport and we're away!"

Then Daniel remembered something, it was Thursday and he had been invited to a party by Johnnie. He's not even sure why he thought of it, he had never been interested in that sort of thing before. Maybe his new lease of life had made him view things differently. Maybe somewhere inside him there was a little kid still striving for attention and wanting to show Helena off like some new toy. Or maybe there was just a part of him that wanted to say goodbye, even if just to a small part of his life. Either way he decided he wanted to go.

"Actually…" he started hesitantly, "…there's this party I've been invited to tonight and I thought that maybe we could go."

"Are you forgetting the rule again, Dan?"

"No it's cool, it's somewhere I've never been before. This guy I work with, sorry *worked* with, Johnnie, well he's always going on about these amazing parties and I've never been to one before. No one would be looking for me there and it could be fun."

Helena thought about this for a moment before relenting. "I guess it would be fun to let my wig down in England one last time. I'm in."

22

They arrived at the party around eight. Daniel had texted Johnnie earlier on asking for the details and had got one of Johnnie's trademark replies that only began to make sense if you imagined them in his voice and re-read them about twenty times.

The party was in a penthouse apartment on the outskirts of town. These particular buildings had only cropped up a few years earlier and Daniel didn't know a single person that could even afford a deposit on them, let alone anyone who actually lived there. He couldn't help but wonder how Johnnie knew anyone with that sort of stature.

Johnnie had told Daniel to give him a missed call when they arrived so he could come let them in and introduce them to some people as Daniel is not "a social genius" as Johnnie said. Dan could have done with Johnnie leaving that part out of his message.

Daniel made the call and true to his word Johnnie appeared a few moments later.

"Maaaaaaaaaaaaaate! So good to see you and whoah!!!" he said, looking at Helena who was sporting a small blue dress and wearing a blonde wig with ringlets in it. "Who the hell is this?" He was coming across as a slack-jawed caveman rather than a social genius right now.

"This," said Daniel with a certain degree of pride, "is my girlfriend Helena."

Helena extended her hand to shake Johnnie's who instead decided to bypass the shake and go for a hand kiss instead. Helena stifled a small shudder.

"Johnnie DeLance," he said, "but you can call me JD, that's what everyone else calls me." In Dan's experience this was a complete fabrication; secretly Dan couldn't wait to expose Johnnie as a huge bullshitter, but for now he just wanted to get his lady a drink.

"You said you were going to introduce us to some people?" he said in an effort to get Johnnie back on task.

"Yeah, man, yeah, let's go. Follow me."

What happened next Daniel did not expect. They entered into the apartment and the atmosphere was buzzing. The whole place was full of convivial people who seemed to fit into two categories, either bohemian or executive looking. There were several medium-sized groups of people and even more small groupings where people were talking heartily. The lighting was low and there was down tempo electro on the stereo; the whole thing was like something you would see in a film where modern high society would converge and bask in their own importance. The most surprising thing of all though was it was EXACTLY how Johnnie had described it. All this time what Daniel thought were tall tales and anecdotes were actually all true.

Johnnie introduced them around to artists, stockbrokers, photographers, sales executives and all manner of other people, some of whose names Daniel vaguely recalled from Johnnie's bragging sessions at work. Helena was the ultimate party guest, she could literally talk to anyone and she constantly regarded Daniel affectionately and helped him to get involved in the conversation where in the past he may have shied away.

He was awestruck watching her, she appeared to seamlessly integrate with everyone around her and she was like a magnet, attracting more and more people to her as the evening drew on. Many of which would then turn to Daniel and tell him what a great catch she was or what a lucky man he was. He couldn't help but agree.

Once Daniel had found his feet a little he left Helena with one of her new friends and Johnnie introduced him to a guy called Steve Reuter, who apparently was looking to hire an extra data analyst for his company and Johnnie had recommended Daniel to him. Though he held no real interest in taking the position Daniel played his part in the conversation but made sure to make reference to his upcoming trip. Steve implored him to get in touch upon his return and Daniel said that he would.

Then his focus in the conversation was stolen by something, or rather someone else in the room. Standing in a doorway at the far end of the room was man in a suit. He had short cropped hair and a couple of days' worth of stubble. He wore his shirt with no tie and the top two buttons undone. There were plenty of other people that looked like this at the party but what made this particular individual remarkable is that his gaze was fixed forcefully on Daniel.

Daniel, not wanting to appear to stare back returned his own focus to Steve but could not stop himself from regularly glancing back at this strange man. Minutes went by and every time Daniel checked he was still staring in his direction.

Steve was talking on about the position and opportunities within the company, information which had Daniel wanted the job he would have needed to pay attention to, if only to save some face at a later date. Daniel's attention however belonged to the man in the doorway.

He looked back one more time and for some unknown reason he glanced down at the floor. Suddenly Daniel was possessed by a phantom from his nightmares. There they were. The purple shoes. Tapping away on the floor. Just like in his dream.

Level headed Daniel wanted to believe it was just a coincidence, but then level headed Daniel had been guilty of being over sceptical about dreams already this week. No, this was conspiracy theorist Daniel's moment now. Clearly they had hacked his phone and could read his messages. The suspicions had to be right and they had to take control.

He broke off the conversation with Steve and scoured the room for Helena; she was nowhere to be seen. It could just be that she was hidden behind a huddle of people, or even in a different room. But no, conspiracy theorist Daniel knew they had taken her, whoever *they* were.

He gave one last hasty look around the room before exiting through the opposite door to which the man was standing. The door led out to a hallway, which in turn led to the entrance of the apartment. There were a few people gathered by the entrance but still no Helena. Daniel made a direct line for the door, pulling his mobile out and attempting to call her. Nothing but the voicemail again.

He was suffocating with panic, why had he left her side? Why had he been so stupid? Why had he even bothered with this party in the first place? He could have just stayed in the hotel with Helena and had another night of room service and sex but no! He had to go and ruin everything.

He pushed past the people blocking the front door and practically forced it open. He glanced over his shoulder and saw the man in purple shoes had made an effort to follow him.

He slammed the door behind him, slowing down his pursuer and pressed the button for the elevator, moments later deciding that it was taking too long and the stairs would be quicker. He was acting erratic and irrational but at least he was acting; that was the first step he thought to regaining control.

He made his way down the stairwell to the ground floor and burst out through the communal entrance. The night air hit him like a train. He jarred his head from side to side looking up and down the street for any sign of Helena, but none could be seen.

Great. He thought. Now they had her God knows where, probably torturing her and all because he had gotten her involved in his pathetic excuse for a life. He wondered why he'd ever allowed himself to hope again.

He felt all the emotions balling up inside him, rising up from his stomach and then for the second time in as many days he found himself vomiting.

He doubled over, heaving onto the pavement, chunks of undigested burger and fries pouring out of him like a sliced open sand bag. He wretched until there was nothing but the lining of his stomach left to wretch up and then he just stood there, staring at his feet and the mess on the floor, panting.

"Waheyyyyy, someone's had too many!" That voice was familiar. It was the unmistakable stretching out of words that could only be Johnnie.

Daniel now turned the blame from himself to Mr DeLance. "Look, mate!" he started, standing up tall and turning round ready to pounce at him with a full blown rant about how Helena had been kidnapped and tortured and it was all his fault. But he never had to say another word because as he turned to see Johnnie he also saw Helena standing behind him.

Safe.

Not kidnapped

Not tortured.

"Dan?" she said quizzically. "What happened?"

"I thought you were… and there was… and then I." he seemed incapable of stringing together a full sentence. "Purple shoes."

"What the hell are you talking about?" This was Johnnie.

"The guy… in purple… shoes." He was still having to breathe between every few words.

"Yeah? What about him?"

"He was fol… following me."

"You mean Carl?"

"I don't… know. He just had purple… shoes."

"Suit? No tie?"

Daniel saved his breath and simply nodded.

"That's Carl, he's a fashion designer, about as gay as they come too, mate, probably just fancied you!" Another pearl of wisdom from the so-called social genius, Daniel thought.

Daniel was not settling for this, his rational side had not yet regained control. There had to be more to it, there simply had to be. Helena on the other hand saw an opportunity to nip all this in the bud and was quick to jump in.

"I think he could probably just do with some rest, Johnnie, it's been an emotional week. Would you mind calling a cab for us, I don't have a number for a company in this area."

"Sure thing, babe," he said with a hint of sleaze.

Once Johnnie was occupied with his task Helena set her full attention to Daniel who now had regained enough breath to start talking properly again.

"There was definitely something dodgy going down in there."

"Don't worry about it, sweetie, it's all going to be fine. Johnnie is calling us a cab and we'll soon be back at the hotel. Then tomorrow we'll be miles away from all this worry. Nothing is going to happen."

He searched her face, it was warm and reassuring, maybe it was all in his head because she didn't look spooked, not one bit. This put him at ease somewhat and he was able to return his focus to how things were rather than wild theories about how they could be.

"I guess you're right, I'm sure I'll feel better once I get back to the hotel and get cleaned up a bit. I can't believe you're still interested in me when you keep seeing me looking like this."

"Well somebody's got to love you." It was said as a joke but Daniel wondered if there was any more weight in her use of the L word.

The taxi didn't take much time to arrive. Johnnie stuck around long enough to ensure they both got in safe and reminded Daniel to call if he needed anything. As they were driving off they heard him shout, "Don't forget to send me a postcard!"

Yeah right, Dan thought, as if anyone sends postcards anymore!

23

When they got back to the hotel Daniel got undressed and jumped into the shower, Helena used the time as an opportunity to pack up some of the room that had served as her home for her extended trip to England.

After he had finished they both climbed into bed together. Daniel asked her endless questions about the places they were about to go and visit and she spoke animatedly about each city. She said that every city has its own character and that she thought those characters get printed on you, so that when you leave, you take a little bit of the city with you.

"You're taking more than just a bit of the city this time," Daniel joked, "you're taking one of the citizens."

She asked him which part of the trip he was most excited about and he said that he couldn't wait to see the Coliseum and the Sistine Chapel in Rome. He returned the question to her and she said she was actually most looking forward to going "back home" and showing off her wonderful Englishman. Daniel was slightly embarrassed but secretly he loved the thought of being a trophy boyfriend.

Then Helena asked him a question that surprised him. She asked him to tell her about his wife.

He was slightly dumbstruck at first, he didn't know where to start. It was impossible for him to recall her without affection and he felt uncomfortable speaking in such a way to his new love. He tried his best to talk about her as he may a friend or a blood relative, rather than a former love. Then when he felt he had answered the question sufficiently he moved the focus to Rachel, his daughter.

He realised that he hadn't given them much thought these last few days and for that he felt a pang of guilt, though not as strong as the one from the park two days previous. This made him realise something.

"Actually," he said, "if there's a chance that we're never coming back then I think I would like the opportunity to say goodbye to them. Would you mind if I visited the cemetery tomorrow?"

"No, not at all. But I'm coming with you, can't have another scare like we did tonight."

"I understand that, but I feel like this is something I need to do alone... you understand right?"

"I do, but I still don't want to let you out of my sight... surely you understand too?"

"OK, how about this? We'll both get taxis tomorrow at the same time, you get yours to the airport and I'll get mine to the cemetery. I'll even pay the guy extra to wait for me so you don't have to worry about me finding another cab and waiting on my own."

She looked on at him, clearly unconvinced. "Plus," he continued, "it will be the middle of the day, with plenty of people there. Nothing will happen then."

Reluctantly Helena gave in, making one last comment that she'd still be happier if Daniel would just let her go too.

They didn't talk anymore that night; instead they just held each other until one by one they fell asleep.

24

The next morning Helena woke with a start. She jumped out of bed and began to pace around frantically, going on about how there was so much to do and absolutely no time to do it.

Daniel decided that if he got himself organised it might make her feel a bit better. He got up, located his backpack and emptied it out onto the bed. In it were a few items of clothes he hadn't yet worn, his passport and the remains of the cash, now seriously depleted by Helena's trip to the travel agents.

He began to repack the bag putting his dirty clothes from the last few days on the bottom and then placing the clean clothes on top of those, remembering to leave something out to wear for the day.

Helena was buzzing in and out of the bedroom, the main room and the bathroom seemingly with no plan of action.

Daniel asked if she would like any help at all but was simply told that a man "wouldn't understand".

She threw a large case onto the bed and began hastily yet somehow neatly placing items in. The case quickly became full and Helena was showing no signs of calming down. Daniel put his hands on her shoulders to hold her still for a moment and then held her in a warm embrace assuring her that everything was going to be OK. This seemed to soothe her a little although she was keen to get things finished.

Once she was packed she let out a large sigh and as if by magic was immediately back to her normal self again.

"I was thinking," Daniel said, "you should take the rest of that cash and get it changed into Euros, or whatever currency we need while you're waiting for me. It's not going to be much use to us as pounds now."

"Yeah, I suppose that would be a good idea. Do you want me to pick anything up for you at the airport while I wait? I'll probably have a quick browse in the shops that are this side of security."

"Nah, I think first step would be for me to buy a bigger case. If we're going to be upping my wardrobe on the road then this backpack won't be up to the task. I'll sort it out when we get to Paris. I'm so excited!"

"Me too!"

Helena did one final sweep of the room to make sure she'd got everything, and then she stood on one spot glancing around and let out another sigh, this one more of sadness than of satisfaction. "I'm really gonna miss this place. You know what I said last night about a city leaving a piece in you? Well I think it works the other way around too, sometimes when you spend enough time somewhere you end up leaving a piece of yourself when you go."

"Well I've spent my whole life here, so God only knows what I'll be leaving!"

She gave a smile with a hint of sorrow behind it and with that they left the room and headed downstairs. Given the length of her stay it would have normally taken a while to check the bill when checking out. Eager to head off however she only gave the five-page invoice a cursory glance and simply handed over her credit card. The staff at the reception expressed their feelings of sadness to see her leave.

They waited outside for their two taxis. When one of them arrived Daniel suggested that Helena take the first one but she insisted on waiting until they were both there. The first driver showed some frustration at this but that soon passed when Helena instructed him to start the meter running.

The second cab arrived around five minutes later. She kissed Daniel sweetly and said, "Be careful, you. See you on the other side."

"Don't worry, I'll be back with you before you even know it. Now that I've found you I'm never letting go."

They kissed again and got into their taxis, Helena in the first one and Daniel in the second. The airport and the cemetery were both in the same general direction from the hotel so they travelled in convoy for a while. When they eventually took their separate routes Helena turned round and blew a kiss to

Daniel through the rear window. Daniel caught it like a scene from a cheesy rom-com.

On the way to the cemetery Daniel cast his thoughts back in time. It was strange, everything that happened before this week seemed like the distant past, as if there was an ocean of years, not days between now and then.

He wanted his goodbye to Izzy and Rachel to honour the women he held in his heart only a few days earlier. They deserved a goodbye from the man they knew, so for a moment he had to leave behind this new Daniel whose heart now belonged so completely to another.

He recalled some of their fonder memories. Their first date at JCs, the day he proposed to her on their trip to the Lake District. Buying their first house together, their wedding day, the day Rachel was born. He drew his thoughts to a halt as they began to approach the accident. He was no longer intent on avoiding pain, but now was a time for reminiscing on happy times, to solidify the last memories he would make of them as happy ones.

There was a funeral procession at the main entrance of the cemetery so the taxi driver elected to drop Daniel off at the smaller entrance around the side. Daniel instructed him to wait and leave the meter running. The driver insisted that he pay at least a portion of the fare upfront as he had "heard this one before". Daniel did so and headed into the cemetery.

He couldn't remember the last time he had visited their graves. It was something he did much less frequently than he thought he should have done but this was just another layer to how he had been protecting himself all these years.

Despite his infrequent visits he had no trouble locating the spot where they were buried. They were both in a single lot and shared a headstone. This had not been done as a way of saving money but Daniel had not liked the idea of Rachel being without her mummy at such a young age. The stone epitaph read:

Isabelle Maria Brody – Loving wife and mother. Gone too soon, forever remembered.

And underneath:

Rachel Annabel Brody – A beautiful Angel who was called home too early.

Daniel stared silently at the grave with his hands in his pockets for several minutes before speaking. When he finally began, his words came slowly.

"Well, my beautiful ladies, I guess you know why I'm here. It looks like without you two here to look after me I got myself in quite a pickle, and that's putting it lightly.

"The truth is, living with you guys was easy. It was so simple to see all the beauty in life when it was reflected in each of your faces; in your smiles, and Rachel, my sweet baby, in your new found laugh, which your mum assured me was wind, but we knew otherwise didn't we, sweetie?

"Then after, well you know after what happened I was left here on my own and the beauty was all gone. I couldn't find it inside myself, all I could find was pain and emptiness.

"I tried to go on, but just didn't know how. Looking back I feel extremely guilty for that and even more so that it has taken someone else to show me the beauty that is inside me, a beauty which I was all too quick to forget that you showed me every day.

"I hope now I have learned to see it for myself."

He paused for a while and thought on this, then concluded it was still too soon to tell. His newfound confidence had come from Helena and it was impossible right now to say how much of it had been sat there waiting the whole time. Even now he had come here determined, knowing what he needed to say and now instead of saying it he had turned inwards again.

Was he really confident? Only the previous day he had been gripped by heavy paranoia the second Helena was out of his sight to which the only catharsis had been her return. His security came from her, not him and what is more, realising this made him realise one other thing. She was not there *now*.

He tried to return his attentions to his goodbye, after all that was his whole reason for being there. But it was now impossible. He was a marked man, and his assailant could be anyone. Any member of the funeral party or any other of the many people here, infiltrating his safety under the guise of a griever.

He glanced around. Jez was everywhere and everyone. From the smallest child to an old man sat in his wheelchair. Everyone needed to be suspected.

Daniel decided if his security came from Helena then the best answer would be to cut his goodbyes short and get back to her. He could find out later how secure he was in himself. When he was in a safer environment and no one was out to kill him.

He looked back to the gravestone and with tears forming in the corners of his eyes softly whispered, "Goodbye."

25

He made his way through the rows of headstones in the direction of the exit, praying fervently that the taxi driver was still there.

He was still suspicious of everyone and he suddenly felt conscious that those around him were aware of how he felt as if he were some sort of radio tower broadcasting out his suspicions for all to hear. Everyone was staring at him, or so he thought as he stumbled towards the exit.

Everywhere he looked he saw the killer. All eyes were on him; they were in it together, all conspiring to bring an end to his life. The world began to spin, the sky and the trees blurring into a turquoise smudge across the horizon. He had felt this way before, but now he couldn't allow it. He had to keep moving, a single pause could be the last nail in his coffin.

Clumsily he tripped over a gravestone and tumbled onto the ground. A nearby groundskeeper saw what had happened and rushed to Daniel's aid, his outstretched hand and courteous efforts however were only regarded with suspicion and contempt. Daniel slapped the man's hand away and got to his feet by himself, barging past the groundskeeper, hell bent on reaching the exit.

The rusty old gates of the side entrance were now in sight. Daniel looked back over his shoulder and could see two men pointing in his direction. Now a sane man would mark this down to the scene Daniel had just caused, but right now sanity was in scarce supply. They were after him, there could be no other explanation.

All he had to do was get through the gate and get in the cab, but wait, how did he know the taxi driver wasn't all part of it too? He could trust no one.

He balled through the gates to where the taxi driver was waiting patiently, leaning against the car. "Ready to go, mate?"

he asked, but without answering Daniel made an abrupt turn to his right and ran off in the direction of the high street.

Without any headstones in place now he quickened his pace, heading at lightning speed for God-knows-where. He broke out onto the high street, but before he turned the corner he glanced one last time over his shoulder. The driver had got back into the taxi and was hot on his tail.

There was no way he could outrun a car, he was barely surviving at his current pace. When he had been a kid there were alleyways behind the shops where the bins had been kept, but since the early 90s access to them had been through gates, which except on collection days were kept locked to keep "undesirables" from loitering about.

He knew he had no choice but to get another taxi, and as ludicrous as it may seem he was much happier placing his trust in a new taxi hailed down on the street over the one from which he had just fled.

He moved out towards the edge of the curb and stuck out his hand. A cab pulled up seconds later and he jumped in, hastily instructing the driver to head to the airport.

"That'll be about thirty quid, mate, is that alright?"

"Yeah," Daniel gasped, "just get me there as soon as you can." Then Daniel had a sudden revelation, it wasn't fine, his money had all been in his bag, which he had left in the other cab.

Thankfully he had his mobile on him, and thankfully he had only taken enough money for the cab ride, the vast majority was still safe with Helena. He gave her a call. One more thing to be grateful for, this time she answered.

"Hey, sweetie, are you on your way?"

"Yeah," he said, still out of breath. "How are you getting on?"

"I'm doing just fine, missing you though. You sound out of breath, is everything alright?"

"Yeah, fine, just had to do a bit of running, I'll tell you all about it when I get there, nothing to worry about.

"Look," he said, before she could ask any more questions, "could I ask you a favour?"

"Sure thing, what can I do?"

"I had to change cabs and my cash is in the other one, could you meet me outside with some money?"

"Yes, no problems. But why did you have to change cabs?"

"It's a long story, as I said I'll explain everything when I'm with you, but all you need to know is I'm OK, I'm in the cab and I'm on my way."

"OK, well just get here as quick as you can, OK?"

"Alright, I'll see you soon. I love you."

There was a moment of silence before the response came back. "I love you too."

The declaration of her affections soothed him a little bit, but his paranoia had not yet subsided. He began to look around again and that's when he noticed that the other taxi driver was still behind them, he had followed them all this way.

Daniel was panicked; he was now even less in control. His taxi would be taking him to the airport where the other driver would easily be able to follow. There was nothing left to do but ride this out and hope that the airport would be busy enough for him to get lost within the crowd.

His heart was racing, he was breathing hard and sweating profusely. It was so hard to know how to feel, each turn the taxi made, each set of lights that turned green brought him closer to his security, his Helena. But at the same time with every passing minute he was getting closer to the end.

The cab pulled into the main airport compound via a roundabout and the other driver was stuck behind a convoy of shuttle buses. This is my chance, Daniel thought. The delay should buy me just enough time to get inside, where it will be busy and safe.

Then he saw her standing there. Outside the departures entrance was the love of his life. The wind blowing through the hair that she had worn on the day they met. The mere sight of her commanding all his fears back in line.

The taxi pulled up and Helena paid the driver. Daniel sprung from the vehicle and threw his arms around her.

"Easy, tiger!" she said.

"I'm just so glad it's all over," he replied, relief instantly washing over him.

"So what happened that got you all flustered?"

"Let's just get inside, I'll tell you everything there."

But before they could make a move, from behind them came the frantic shouts of the other driver. "Hey, you, hey! Hey! Hey!"

"Isn't that the other driver?" asked Helena looking puzzled.

"Yeah, quick, let's just go and get inside, come on!"

"But he's got your bag!"

"My wha..." Daniel started, but he too turned to look at the flustered driver to see that he was carrying Daniel's backpack.

"You forgot your bag, mate," he said as Daniel gazed at him sheepishly. "Oh, and you owe me another twenty quid!"

Daniel couldn't help himself; he just burst out laughing, practically doubled over.

"Look, mate," the taxi driver went on, "this isn't funny, I had to drive the whole way across town for this, and you're just gonna laugh at me? Last time I do a good deed!"

"I'm sorry," Daniel said, still in fits of laughter, "but you would never believe what I was thinking!"

"Yeah OK, I'm a taxi driver, I've heard it all, mate. Now have you got my twenty quid?"

Helena could see that Daniel was preoccupied with his fit of the giggles so she produced another £20 note and gave it to the driver, who, satisfied with being paid, returned to his cab and left them alone.

"So what the hell was all that about?" Helena asked, determined to get to the bottom of Daniel's strange behaviour.

"I thought he was trying to kill me!" This sentence seemed to kick him into full-blown hysterics and Helena stared on as Daniel held his stomach tight, bellowing with laughter.

It all seemed so ludicrous now; the simple idea that the taxi driver could be in on it all. He thought back about all these paranoid acts and they all had one thing in common, nothing had actually happened. It was all in his head. He was here, he was safe and he was with Helena.

"So," she said in an effort to interrupt his laughter, "are you going to tell me what happened? Or do I have to stand here all day?"

He composed himself and told her about his ordeal. About how he had suspected everyone in the cemetery and then later fled from the taxi driver.

"Anyway," he concluded, "everything is going to be fine now. We're going to get on the plane and head to where no one even knows who I am. No more looking over my shoulder, no more suspecting everyone of foul play. I'm with you now. I'm safe."

She took one look at him and asked, "What makes you think you're safe with me?"

This nearly forced him to burst out into laughter again, but the look on her face was serious, not jovial. Before he had a chance to analyse the situation any further she threw her arms around him, confusing him even further.

Then he felt something peculiar. She was not holding him tight, like in a lovers embrace, her arms were outstretched and there was something sharp and warm, pricking him in the back. Like a mosquito, but much, much larger.

He was overcome with confusion; the world began to lose colour and sounds started to blur into one. He was discombobulated and he searched within himself for a word, help perhaps, but all that came was, "Why?"

She moved her head back and looked him in the eyes, the woman he had known no longer present in her face.

"Why?" he said again, fighting to push out the words. "Why did you let me fall in love with you, if you were going to kill me? If it was you all along."

"Daniel, Daniel, Daniel." Her accent had completely vanished and once again Daniel was at a loss to say where she was from. "If I'd have just left you how you were, then there would have been nothing in it for me. It was never about the money, although thank you for all the extra cash that you literally threw in my direction. Don't you see, Daniel? Before taking a life, the life needs to be worth taking." Her voice was cold and calculating, just like the stranger in the hospital.

He tried to say something back but he could already feel his limbs going numb. His body felt heavy on his legs and she walked him to a nearby bench, where when she loosened her grip slightly, he sank into a slump.

She stared at him one last time and then turned to walk away. To her these days had been nothing but a game. Daniel may not be able to feel his body, but he could not escape the pain of his heart shattering into a million pieces.

The last thing Daniel Brady ever did in his life was to try and hold his head high. But as the poison took hold, his head sank to his chest and just before his eyes closed for the last time he saw her walking away. The woman in the purple shoes.